Christmas Miracles in Maternity

*Hope, magic and precious new beginnings
at Teddy's!*

Welcome to Teddy's Centre for Babies and Birth, where the brightest stars of neonatal and obstetric medicine work tirelessly to save tiny lives and deliver bundles of joy all year round—but there's never a time quite as magical as Christmas!

Although the temperature might be dropping outside, unexpected surprises are heating up for these dedicated pros! And as Christmas Day draws near secrets are revealed, hope is ignited and love takes over.

Cuddle up this Christmas with the heart-warming stories of the doctors, nurses, midwives and surgeons at Teddy's in the **Christmas Miracles in Maternity** mini-series:

Available November 2016

The Nurse's Christmas Gift
by Tina Beckett

The Midwife's Pregnancy Miracle
by Kate Hardy

Available December 2016

White Christmas for the Single Mum
by Susanne Hampton

A Royal Baby for Christmas
by Scarlet Wilson

Dear Reader,

Have you ever wanted something so badly that it consumes your every waking thought? And yet that very same desire ends up causing unimaginable pain?

Annabelle Brookes finds herself facing a tragic cycle of hope and grief as she tries time and time again to carry a child to term. Those failed attempts finally affect her health and her relationship with her husband. When he finally puts his foot down and says, 'No more', she is devastated. So devastated that she pushes him away.

Years later Annabelle comes face-to-face with the man she once loved. All the emotions she thought long-dead are resurrected, and she has to decide once and for all what the important things in life are. Only this is Christmas, the season of miracles, when nothing is carved in stone.

Thank you for joining Max and Annabelle as they struggle to let go of the pain of the past. And maybe—just maybe—they'll discover something more tucked among the tinsel and the holiday lights. I hope you enjoy reading their story as much as I loved writing it!

Love,_

Tina Beckett

THE NURSE'S CHRISTMAS GIFT

BY
TINA BECKETT

MILLS
BOON®

First published in Great Britain 2016
By Mills & Boon, an imprint of HarperCollins*Publishers*
1 London Bridge Street, London, SE1 9GF

Large Print edition 2017

© 2016 Harlequin Books S.A.

Special thanks and acknowledgement are given to Tina Beckett for her contribution to the Christmas Miracles in Maternity series

ISBN: 978-0-263-06695-1

Our policy is to use papers that are natural, renewable and recyclable products and made from wood grown in sustainable forests. The logging and manufacturing processes conform to the legal environmental regulations of the country of origin.

Printed and bound in Great Britain
by CPI Antony Rowe, Chippenham, Wiltshire

Three-times Golden Heart® finalist
Tina Beckett learned to pack her suitcases almost before she learned to read. Born to a military family, she has lived in the United States, Puerto Rico, Portugal and Brazil. In addition to travelling, Tina loves to cuddle with her pug, Alex, spend time with her family and hit the trails on her horse. Learn more about Tina from her website, or 'friend' her on Facebook.

Books by Tina Beckett

Mills & Boon Medical Romance

The Hollywood Hills Clinic
Winning Back His Doctor Bride

Midwives On-Call at Christmas
Playboy Doc's Mistletoe Kiss

To Play with Fire
His Girl From Nowhere
How to Find a Man in Five Dates
The Soldier She Could Never Forget
Her Playboy's Secret
Hot Doc from Her Past
A Daddy for Her Daughter

Visit the Author Profile page
at millsandboon.co.uk for more titles.

To my kids,
who are always willing to give me space—and
time—when I'm under deadline. I love you!

**Praise for
Tina Beckett**

'The book had everything I want from a
medical romance and so much more…
Tina Beckett has shown that the world of
romance mixed with the world of medical can
be just as hot, just as *wow* and just as addictive
as any other form of romance read out there.'
—*Contemporary Romance Reviews* on
To Play with Fire

'Tina Beckett has the ability to take me
on a journey of romance so strong and so
mind-blowing it feels like I am floating on
cloud nine for weeks afterward. This time
she has certainly done it again!'
—*Contemporary Romance Reviews* on
How to Find a Man in Five Dates

CHAPTER ONE

MAX AINSLEY WAS happy to be back on familiar soil.

Opening the door to his new cottage in a brand-new city, he hefted his duffel bag and tossed it over his shoulder, enjoying the warmth he found inside. Six months was too long; the days and nights spent helping displaced children in war-ravaged North Africa had eaten into his soul—one painful bite at a time. Trying to meet each desperate need had drained his emotional bank account until there was nothing left. He'd needed to come back to recharge and decide what he wanted to do next.

What better season than winter? The icy weather and the festive lights of the approaching holiday should help him push aside the thoughts of what he hadn't been able to accomplish on this trip. At least he hoped so.

Three years of running from his past had changed nothing. Maybe it was time to start living in the present. To sign the papers he'd left behind and to finally let go of the past once and for all.

Shedding his parka and throwing his belongings onto a nearby leather sofa with a sigh, he surveyed the place. With its white-painted walls and comfortable furniture, it wasn't huge or fancy, but it was big enough for a landing place, at least until he could figure out where he wanted to park his butt for the long haul. Sienna McDonald had sent pictures of several possibilities that were just a short distance from the hospital, and he'd settled on this one, the cottage's quaint one-bedroom floor plan made more attractive by the small private garden off the back. This was the place.

He could finally sell his flat back in London. And maybe it was time to call his solicitor and have him complete the process—to cut any remaining ties with a certain dark period in his life.

He spied a piece of paper on the table in the dining room and stiffened, before he realised it couldn't be from her. She had no idea where he was right now. And she hadn't tried to find him over the last couple of years. At least not that he knew of.

Wandering over to the note, he placed a finger on the pink stationery and cocked his head as he made out the cheerful words.

'Welcome to Cheltenham and to Teddy's! I've put some milk, cheese and cold meat in the fridge, and there is bread and sweets in the cupboard along with some other staples to help get you started. The boiler is lit, instructions are on the unit. I hope you're ready to work, because I am more than ready for a rest!'

She'd signed her name with a flourish at the end.

Sweets, eh? That made him smile. But he was

glad for the boiler, as snow was expected to hit any day and the temperatures had been steadily dropping. His body was still trying to adjust to the chill after all those months dealing with the hot temperatures of Sudan.

He was due at Teddy's in the morning to start his contract, replacing Sienna McDonald when she went on maternity leave. She'd sent him a letter as he was packing for the flight telling him to get ready for a wild ride. There was a winter virus running through the halls of the hospital, affecting patients and staff alike. They were short-staffed and overworked.

He was ready. Anything to keep his mind off his previous life.

And the timing couldn't have been more perfect. Sienna would be there to show him the ropes, and Max would have time to adjust to being back in a modern hospital, where day-to-day life was not always a life and death struggle.

Well, that was not entirely true. In the world of paediatric cardiothoracic medicine, things were often about life and death, but they were caused by the battle raging within the person's body, not the cruel deeds done by one human against another. And with Doctors Without Borders, he had seen his share of war and the horrific results of it.

His mind headed to a darker place, and Max forced it back to the mundane tasks he had to accomplish before his first shift tomorrow morning: shave the scruff of several weeks off his face, unpack, hunt down a vehicle to use.

With that in mind, he headed to the refrigerator to find something to eat. And then he would face the day, and hopefully get ready to face his future…and his first step towards banishing the past, once and for all.

Annabelle Brookes couldn't believe how crowded the ward was. All the beds were full, and patients were seemingly crammed into every nook and cranny. The winter virus was not only sending people flooding into the hospital, but it was sending staff flooding out—multiple nurses and doctors had all become ill over the past several days. So far she had steered clear of its path, but who knew how long that would hold? She was frankly exhausted and, with six hours left to her shift, she was sure she would be dead on her feet by the time she headed home.

Despite it all, she was glad Ella O'Brien had pestered her until she'd agreed to come to Cheltenham a year ago. Maybe because her friend had recognised the signs of depression and the deadly spiral her life had taken after her husband had left for parts unknown. Whatever it had been, Annabelle felt she was finally getting her life back under control. She had Ella to thank for that. And for helping her land this plum position.

Head neonatal nurse was a dream come true for her. She might not be able to have children of her own, but she was happy to be able to rock, hold and treat other people's babies all day long. Working at the same hospital as her midwife friend also meant there was plenty of time for girlie outings and things to take her mind off her own problems.

She let her fingers run across a draping of tinsel against a doorway as she went by, the cool slide of glittery metal helping relax her frazzled nerves.

Tucking a strand of hair back into the plait that ran halfway down her back, she dodged people and patients alike as she made her way towards the nursery and her next patient: Baby Doe, aka Baby Hope.

The baby had been abandoned by her mother—who was little more than a baby herself—and Annabelle felt a special affinity with this tiny creature. After all, hadn't Annabelle been dumped by the person who should have loved her the most but left her languishing with a broken heart? No. Actually, Annabelle had done the dumping, but her heart had still splintered into pieces.

Baby Hope's heart was literally broken, whereas Annabelle's was merely…

She stiffened her jaw. No. Her heart was just fine, thank you very much.

Was that why that paperwork was still sitting on a shelf gathering dust? And it was too. Annabelle had cleaned around the beige envelope over the past couple of years, but hadn't been able to bring herself to touch it, much less open it and read the contents. Because she already knew what they said. She had been the one to do the filing.

But Max had never responded. Or sent his signed copy back to her solicitor.

And if he had? What then?

She had no idea.

As she rounded the nurses' station to check the schedule and see what other cases she'd been assigned for the day, the phone rang. A nurse sitting behind the desk picked up the phone, waving at her as she answered the call.

'Baby Doe? Oh, yes, Annabelle just arrived. I'll send her in.' She set the phone down.

Maybe the first order of business after her divorce should be to officially get rid of her married name. It still hurt to have it attached to her, even though she no longer went by Annabelle Ainsley.

'Miss McDonald and her replacement are doing rounds and are ready to examine the baby. Do you mind filling them in on what's happened over the last few hours?'

'On my way.' Annabelle had already been headed towards the glass window that made up the viewing area of the special care baby unit, so it was perfect timing. Arriving on the floor, she spotted a heavily pregnant Sienna McDonald ducking into the room. The neonatal cardiothoracic surgeon had been overseeing Baby Doe's care as they waited for an available heart for the sick infant. Another man, wearing a lab coat and sporting dark washed jeans, went in behind Sienna. She could only catch a glimpse of a strong back and thick black hair, but something inside her took a funny little turn at the familiar way the man moved.

Shaking her head to clear it, she reached the door a few seconds later and slid inside.

She headed towards the baby's cot, finding Sienna and the other doctor—their backs to her—hovering over it.

About to step around to the other side, the stranger raised the top of the unit. 'Her colour doesn't look good.'

Annabelle stifled a gasp, stopping in her tracks for several horrified seconds. She lifted her eyes and stared at the man's back.

That voice.

Those gruff masculine tones were definitely not the feminine Scottish lilt belonging to Sienna, that was for sure. This had to be Sienna's replacement. Had she actually seen the name of the new doctor written somewhere? She didn't think so, but she was beginning to think she should have paid more attention.

She swallowed down the ball of bile before the pressure built to dangerous levels.

The new doctor spoke again. 'What's her diagnosis?'

The ball in Annabelle's throat popped back into place with a vengeance.

It couldn't be.

Sienna glanced over at him. 'Hypoplastic left heart syndrome. She's waiting on a donor heart.'

The other doctor's dark head bent as he examined the baby. 'How far down is she on the list?'

'Far enough that we're all worried. Especially Annabelle Brookes—you'll meet her soon. She's the nurse who's been with our little patient from the time she was born.'

Annabelle, who had begun sliding back towards the door, stopped when the new doctor slowly lifted his head, turning it in her direction. Familiar brown eyes she would recognise anywhere met hers and narrowed, staring for what seemed like an eternity but had to have been less than a second. There wasn't the slightest flinch in his expression. She could have been a complete stranger.

But she wasn't.

He knew very well who she was. And she knew him.

No. It couldn't be.

For a soul-searing moment she wondered if she'd been mistaken, that he wasn't Sienna's replacement at all, but was here to say he'd finally signed the papers. Maybe he'd heard about Baby Hope's case and had just popped in to take a look while they hunted for Annabelle.

Or...maybe he'd met someone else.

Her whole system threatened to shut down as she stood there staring.

'Annabelle? Are you all right?' Sienna's voice startled her enough to force her to blink.

'Oh, yes, I...um...' What was she supposed to say?

Max evidently didn't have that problem. He came away from Hope's incubator, extending his hand. 'I didn't realise you'd moved from London.'

'Yes. I did.' She ignored his hand, tipping her chin just a fraction, instead. So he hadn't come here to find her.

Sienna glanced from one to the other. 'You two already know each other?'

One side of Max's mouth turned up in a semblance of a smile as he allowed his hand to drop back by his side. 'Quite well, actually.'

Yes, they knew each other. But 'quite well'? She'd thought so at one time. But in the end… Well, he hadn't stuck around.

Of course, she'd been the one to tell him to go. And he had. Without a single attempt to change her mind—or to fight for what they'd once had.

Sienna's brows went up, obviously waiting for some kind of explanation. But what could she say, really?

She opened her mouth to try to save the situation, but a shrill noise suddenly filled the room.

An alarm! And this one wasn't in her head.

All eyes swivelled back to Baby Hope, who lay still in her incubator.

It was the pulse oximeter. Hope wasn't breathing!

'Let's get some help in here!' Max was suddenly belting out orders in a tone that demanded immediate response.

Glancing again at the baby's form, she noted that the tiny girl's colour had gone from bad to worse, a dangerous mottling spreading over her nappy-clad form. Annabelle's heart plummeted, her fingers beginning a familiar tingle that happened every time she went into crisis mode.

Come on, little love. Don't do this. Not when we're just getting to know each other.

Social services had asked Annabelle to keep a special eye on the infant, since she had no next of kin who were willing to take on her care. Poor little thing.

Annabelle knew what it was like to feel alone.

In Max's defence, it had been her choice. But he had issued an ultimatum. One she hadn't been prepared to accept.

Right now, though, all she needed to think about was this little one's battle for life. Max shot

Sienna a look. The other doctor nodded at him. Whatever the exchange was, Max took the lead.

'We need to tube her.'

Annabelle went to the wall and grabbed a pair of gloves from the dispenser, shoving her hands into them and forcing herself to take things one step at a time. To get ahead of yourself was to make a mistake.

She hurried to get the trach tube items, tearing into sterile packages with a vengeance. Two more nurses rushed into the room, hearing the cries for help. Each went to work, knowing instinctively what needed to be done. They'd all been through this scenario many times before.

But not with Baby Hope.

Annabelle moved in next to Max and handed him each item as he asked for it, her mind fixed on helping the tiny infant come back from the precipice.

Trying not to count the seconds, she watched Max in motion, marvelling at the steadiness of his large hands as he intubated the baby, his face

a mask of concentration. A look that was ach-
ingly familiar. She swallowed hard. She needed
to think of him as a doctor. Not as someone she'd
once loved.

And lost.

He connected the tubing to the ventilator as
one of the other nurses set the machine up and
switched it on.

Almost immediately, Baby Hope's chest rose
and fell in rhythmic strokes as the ventilator did
the breathing for her. As if by magic, the pulse
ox alarm switched off and the heart-rate monitor
above the incubator began sounding a steadier
blip-blip-blip as the heart reacted to the life-
giving oxygen.

The organ was weak, but at least it was beating.

But for how much longer?

Thank God they hadn't needed to use the paddles to shock it back into rhythm. Baby Hope
was already receiving prostaglandin to prevent
the ductus in her heart from closing and cutting

off blood flow. And they had her on a nitrogen/ oxygen mix in an attempt to help the oxygen move to the far reaches of her body. But even so, her hands and extremities were tinged blue, a sure sign of cyanosis. It would only get worse the longer she went without a transplant.

'She's back in rhythm.'

At least a semblance of rhythm, and she wasn't out of the woods, not by a long shot. Her damaged heart—caused by her mum's drug addiction—was failing quickly. Without a transplant, she would die. Whether that last crisis arrived in a week or two or three, the outcome would be the same.

Annabelle sent up a silent prayer that a donor heart would become available.

Even as she prayed it, though, she hated the fact that another family would have to lose their child so that Baby Hope might live.

They watched a few more minutes as things settled down. 'We'll leave her on the ventilator until we figure out exactly what happened. We can try adjusting the nitrogen rate or play with some of her other meds to see if we can buy her a little more time.'

Sienna nodded. 'I was thinking the exact thing.' She glanced at Annabelle. 'Are you okay?'

It was the second time she'd asked her that question. And the second time she had trouble coming up with a response.

'I will be.'

'I know this one's special to you.'

Of course. Sienna was talking about the baby. Not about Max and his sudden appearance back in her life.

'I just want her to have a chance.'

'As stubborn as you are, she has it.' Sienna gave her a smile.

'Annabelle is nothing, if not tenacious.' Max's voice came through, only there wasn't a hint of amusement in the words. And she knew why. Because he wasn't referring to Hope. He was referring to how she'd clung to what she'd thought was *their* dream only to find out it wasn't.

'You said you know each other?'

When Annabelle came to work this morning, never in her wildest imaginings had she pictured this scene. Because she already knew how it was going to play out. She braced herself for impact.

'We do.'

There was a pause as the other doctor waited to be enlightened.

Annabelle tried to head it off, even though she knew it was hopeless. 'We've known each other for years.'

'Yes,' Max murmured. 'You could say that. Your Annabelle Brookes is actually Annabelle Ainsley. My wife.'

'Your...' Sienna suddenly looked as if she'd rather be anywhere else but here. 'It didn't even dawn on me. Your names...'

'Are not the same. I know.' Max's mouth turned down at the corners, a hard line that she recognised forming along the sides of his jaw.

'I see you've gone back to your maiden name.' He pinned her with a glance.

'We're separated. Getting a divorce.' She explained as quickly as she could without adding that going back to her maiden name had been a way to survive the devastation that his leaving had caused.

Even though you're the one who asked him to go.

They hadn't spoken since the day he'd found her temperature journal and realised that, although she'd stopped doing the in-vitro procedures as he'd demanded, she hadn't completely given up hope. Until that very minute.

When she'd seen the look on his face as he'd thumbed through the pages, she'd known it was over. She'd grabbed the book from his hands and told him to leave.

And just like that, he'd walked out of their front door and out of her life.

Just like Baby Hope's mother.

And like that lost soul, Max had never come back.

Until now.

She frowned. 'Did you know I was at Teddy's when you accepted that contract to take Sienna's position?'

Even as she asked it, she knew it made no sense for him to have come here. Not without a good reason.

Like those papers on her shelf?

'No.'

That one curt word told her everything she needed to know. If he'd known she was working at the Royal Cheltenham, this was the last place he'd have chosen to come.

Sienna touched a gloved hand to the baby's head. 'If you two can finish getting her stabilised, I need to get off my feet for a few minutes.' She eyed Max. 'Why don't you give me a call when you're done here and I'll finish showing you around the hospital?'

'Sounds good. Thanks.'

Annabelle was halfway surprised that he hadn't just said he was ready now. He had to be as eager to get away from her as she was to get away from him. But they had their patient to consider.

Their?

Oh, God. If he was Sienna's replacement, that meant they would share this particular case. And others like it.

As soon as Sienna had left the room along with the other nurses, Max took a few moments to finish going over the baby's chart, making notes in it while Annabelle squirmed. She couldn't believe he was here. After all this time.

And for the tiniest second, when those intelligent eyes of his had swept over her, she'd entertained the thought that maybe he really had come here looking for her. But it was obvious from his behaviour that he hadn't.

He hadn't seemed all that pleased that she'd dumped his name. How could he expect otherwise, though? She'd wanted no reminders of their time together, not that a simple name change could ever erase all the pain and sadness over the way their marriage had ended.

'Why don't you fill me in on the details of her care? Miss McDonald seemed to indicate you know the baby better than anyone else on staff.' The cool way he asked the question made heat rush to her face.

Here she was agonising over the past, while he was able, as always, to wall off his feelings and emotions. It had driven her crazy when they were together that he could behave as if their world weren't imploding as she'd had miscarriage after miscarriage.

'Social services needed someone who could report back to them on what was happening with her care. And since I'm head nurse, it kind of fell to me to do it.'

'Somehow I didn't think you would remain a neonatal nurse. Not after everything that happened.'

She shrugged. 'I love my job. Just because I can't…have children doesn't mean I want to go into another line of nursing. I'm not one to throw in the towel.'

'I think that depended on the situation.' His words had a hard edge to them.

She decided to take a page from his book and at least try to feign indifference. 'What do you want me to tell you about her?'

'Do you know anything about her history? Her mother?'

Annabelle filled him in on everything she could, from the fact that Baby Hope's mother had been hooked on heroin to the fact that she'd fled the hospital soon after giving birth, staff only discovering her absence when they went in to take her vitals. They'd found her bed empty, her hospital gown wadded up under the covers. They'd called the authorities, but in the two weeks since the baby's birth no one had come forward with any information.

The drug use had caused the baby to go through withdrawals in addition to the in-utero damage her heart had sustained. It was getting weaker by the day. In fact, every ounce she gained put more strain on it. Normally in these children, Annabelle considered weight gain something to be celebrated. Not in Hope's case. It just meant she had that much less time to live.

'Does any of that help?' she asked.

'It does. I'm going to up her dose of furosemide and see if we can get a little of that fluid off her belly. I think that's why she stopped breathing. If it's not any better in an hour or two, I'm going to try to draw some of it off manually.'

'We did that a few days ago. It seemed to help.'

'Good.'

They looked at each other for a long moment, then Max said, 'You've let your hair grow.'

The unexpectedness of the observation made her blink. 'It makes it easier to get out of the way.'

Annabelle used to tame her waves rather than pulling them back. Between blowing them out and using a straightening iron, she'd spent a lot of time on her appearance. Once Max had left, though, there'd seemed little reason to go through those contortions any more. It was only when she stopped that she realised she'd been simply going through the motions for the last half of their marriage. Having a baby had become such a priority that her every waking moment had been consumed with it. It was no wonder he'd jumped at the chance to get out. She hadn't liked who she'd become either.

She opened her mouth to say something more, before deciding the less personal they made their interactions, the better for both of them. They'd travelled down that road once before and it hadn't ended well. And she definitely didn't want to give him the impression that she'd been pining for him over the past three years. She hadn't been. She'd got well and truly over him.

'Since you're working here now, maybe we should set down some ground rules to avoid any sticky situations.' She paused. 'Unless you'd like to change your mind about staying.'

His eyes narrowed. 'I signed a contract. I intend to abide by the terms of it.'

Was that why he hadn't moved to complete the process of terminating their union? Because he viewed their marriage as a contract rather than an emotional commitment? She'd been the one to actually file, not him.

Her throat clogged at the thought, but she pushed ahead, needing to finish their conversation so she could leave. Before the crazy avalanche of emotions buried her any deeper.

'Most people at Teddy's don't know that I was married. They just assume I'm single. All except for Ella.'

Since she no longer wore her ring, it made it that much easier to assume she had no one in her life.

His brows went up. 'Ella O'Brien?'

'Yes.' He would know who Ella was. They'd been best friends for years. She was very surprised her friend hadn't got wind of Max's arrival. Then again, maybe Annabelle would have known had she paid more attention during staff meetings. She'd known Sienna was going on maternity leave soon but had had no idea that Max was the one who'd be taking her place. Maybe because Baby Hope had taken up most of her thoughts in the last couple of weeks.

'How is she?'

'Ella? She's fine.' She looked away from him, reaching down to touch Hope's tiny hand over the side of the still-open incubator. 'Anyway, Ella knows about us, but, as you could see from Sienna's reaction, that information hasn't made its way around the hospital. I would appreciate if you didn't go around blurting out that you're my husband. Because you're not. You haven't been for the last three years.'

One side of his mouth went up in that mouth-watering way that used to make her tremble. But right now, she was desperate to put this runaway train back on its tracks.

'I have a paper that says otherwise.'

'And I have one that says I'm ready to be done with that part of my life.'

'The divorce papers. I'm surprised you haven't followed up on them with your solicitor.'

She should have had that solicitor hound Max until he signed, but she hadn't, and she wasn't quite sure why. 'I've been busy.'

His eyes went to Hope. 'I can see that.'

'So you'll keep our little…situation between us?'

'How do you know Miss McDonald isn't going to say something to someone?'

'She won't.' Sienna was secretive enough about her own past that Annabelle was pretty sure privacy was a big deal to the other doctor.

'And Ella? You don't think she'll say anything?'

'Not if she knows what's good for her.' She said it with a wryness in her voice, because her friend was obstinate to the point of stubbornness about some things. But she was a good and faithful friend. She'd mothered Annabelle when she'd come to her crying her eyes out when Max had walked out of the door. No, Ella wouldn't tell anyone.

Annabelle pulled her hand from the incubator and took a deep breath. Then she turned back to face Max again.

'Please. Can't we try to just work together like the professionals we are? At least for the time you're here.' She wanted to ask exactly how long that would be, but for now she had to assume it was until Sienna was finished with her maternity leave. If she thought of it as a finite period of time she could survive his presence. At least she hoped she could.

But she already knew she'd be seeing a lot more of him. Especially if he was going to be the doctor who either opened Hope's chest and placed a donor heart in it or who signed her death certificate.

She closed her eyes for a second as the remembered sound of that alarm sliced through her being. How long before that sound signalled the end of a life that had barely begun?

'I don't know, Anna.' His low voice caused her lids to wrench apart. 'Can we?'

Her name on his lips sent a shiver through her, as did his words. It was the first time she'd heard the shortened version of Annabelle in three years. In fact, during their very last confrontation he'd reverted to her full name. And then he was gone.

So it made her senses go wonky to hear the drawled endearment murmured in something other than anger.

She'd wanted a simple answer…a promise that Max would do his best to keep their time together peaceful. He hadn't given her that. Or maybe he was simply acknowledging something that she was afraid to admit: that it was impossible for them to work together as if they'd never crossed paths before. Because they had.

And if those old hurts and resentments somehow came out with swords drawn?

Then, as much as she wanted to keep their past relationship in the past, it would probably spill over into the present in a very real way.

CHAPTER TWO

'AND THIS IS where all of that wonderful hospital food is prepared.'

Sienna's easy smile wasn't able to quite penetrate the shock to his system caused by seeing Anna standing over that incubator. Why hadn't he kept track of where she was?

Because he hadn't wanted to know. Knowing meant he had to do something about those papers her solicitor had sent him. And he hadn't been ready to. Maybe fate was forcing his hand. Making him finally put an end to that part of his life in order to move forward to the next phase.

Wasn't that part of the reason he'd come home? To start living again?

Yes, but he hadn't meant to do it quite like this.

He decided the best way to take his mind

off Anna was to put it on something...or someone else.

'The ubiquitous hospital food.' He allowed his
mouth to quirk to the side. 'But it's probably better than what I've been eating for the past six
months.'

She laughed. 'I'm sure Doctors Without Borders feeds you pretty decently.' She paused to
look at him as they made their way down the
corridor. 'What was it like over there?'

'Hard. Lots of pressing needs, and not knowing where to start. Not being able to meet all of
those needs was a tough pill to swallow.' Memories of desperate faces played through his head
like a slide show. Those he saved...and those he
couldn't.

'I can imagine it was. And living in another
country for months at a time? It couldn't have
been easy being away from the comforts of
home.'

'I heard you had a little experience with that
as well. What was the kingdom of Montanari

like?' Someone had mentioned that the other cardiothoracic surgeon had visited the tiny country on an extended stay, but that she had returned quite suddenly.

Sienna stared straight ahead. 'It was different.'

Different. In other words, move on to another subject. He was happy to oblige, since he knew of one particular subject he was just as eager to avoid. 'How about your cases here? Anything interesting?'

The other doctor's shoulders relaxed, and she threw him a smile that seemed almost grateful. 'Well, we actually have a mum who is expecting quadruplets. We're keeping an extra-close eye on her but so far she's doing well and the babies are all fine.'

'That's good.' He didn't ask any more questions. Someone carrying that many foetuses made him think of fertility treatments—another subject he wasn't eager to explore.

'Apparently they might bring in a world-renowned neonatal specialist if any complications develop.'

How many times would he have loved to fly in a specialist when he was in Africa? But, of course, there were only those, like him, who had volunteered their time and expertise. Doctors Without Borders sometimes took pot luck as far as who was willing to go. As a result there were often holes in treatment plans, or a patient who needed help from a specialist that wasn't on site. That was when the most heartbreaking scenarios occurred.

Yet despite that he was already missing those brief, and often frantic, interactions with the team in Sudan, which surprised him given how exhausted he'd been by the end. Or maybe it was the shock of having to work with Annabelle that had him wishing he could just fly back to Africa and a life where long-term connections with other people were neither expected nor desired. It was more in line with the way he'd grown up. And far removed from what he'd once had with

Anna. He'd decided that keeping his distance from others was the safer route.

'Who is the specialist?'

'Hmm…someone told me, but I can't remember her name. I do remember it's a woman. I'd have to look.' She stopped in front of a set of double doors. 'And this is where we work our magic.'

The surgical unit. The epicentre of Max's—and Sienna's—world. Even with all the prep work that went on before the actual surgery, this was still where everything would be won or lost. Annabelle had once said she didn't know how he did it. He wasn't completely sure either. He just did it. The same way she did her job, standing beside the incubators of very sick babies and taking the best care she could of them.

Why was he even thinking about Annabelle right now? 'Can we go inside?'

'Of course.' She hit a button on the wall and the doors swung wide to allow them through. Glancing at the schedule on the whiteboard at the nurses' station, she said, 'Do you want to scrub up and observe a surgery? There's a gall-bladder being taken out in surgical unit two.'

'No, I'm good. But I would like to observe your next cardiac surgery.'

Sienna gave a sigh and put a hand to her belly. 'Sure, but I'm really hoping to scale back by about seventy-five per cent over the next week so I can leave without worrying that you haven't carried an actual caseload.'

Maybe he should have been offended by that, but he wasn't. Sienna didn't know him from Adam. He was pretty sure that she could still carry her share of the patient load, but her comment had been more about wanting to see him in action. To reassure herself that she was leaving her little charges in the best possible hands. He was determined not to disappoint her.

'That sounds fair enough.' He paused. 'And the baby who was in crisis? Baby...Hope?'

'She doesn't have an official name. Hope is Annabelle's pet name for her. I think it's a fingers-crossed kind of thing. Whatever it is, it's stuck, and we all find ourselves calling her that now.'

That sounded just like Annabelle. Refusing to give up hope, even when it was obvious that the procedures were not going to work.

'Annabelle mentioned social services. And that the mum took off?'

'Yes. The mum came in while she was in labour. She was an addict and abandoned the baby soon afterwards. We have no idea where she is.'

Max's chest tightened. His parents had never actually abandoned him physically, except for those long cruises and trips they'd taken, leaving him in the care of an aunt. But emotionally?

'Anyway,' Sienna went on, 'I'm assigning the case to you. Make sure you become familiar with it. Your best bet for doing that is to get with Annabelle and go over her patient file. She has followed that baby from the beginning. She knows more about her than anyone, maybe even me, and I'm Baby Hope's doctor.'

Max's heart twinged out a warning. The last thing he wanted to do was spend even more time with Annabelle, because it was…

Dangerous.

But what else could he do? Say no? Tell Sienna that he couldn't be a professional when it came to dealing with his almost-ex? Not hardly.

Maybe Sienna saw something in his face. 'Is that going to be a problem considering the circumstances? I'm sorry, I had no idea you two even knew each other.'

If there was one thing Max was good at, it was disengaging his brain from his heart.

'It won't be a problem.'

'Good.'

He'd work with Anna. Until it was over. Because one way or the other it would be. The baby would either have a new heart, or she wouldn't. The twinge he'd felt seconds earlier grew to an ache—just like the one he'd dealt with on an almost daily basis while working in the Sudan.

He rubbed a palm over the spot for a second to ease the pressure.

'How often do hearts come available?'

'Do you mean here in Cheltenham? Some years there are more. Some years, less.'

'How many transplants have you done?'

'One. In my whole career. We deal with lots of holes in the heart and diverting blood flow, but hypoplastic cases are rare at Teddy's.'

So why was she handing the case over to him? This was a chance that she'd just admitted didn't come across her desk very often. 'Are you sure you don't want it?'

'Very.' Something flashed through her brown eyes. A trickle of fear? His gaze shifted lower. Was she worried about the health of her own baby?

He remembered well the worry over whether a foetus would make it to term. In fact he remembered several times when he'd prayed over Annabelle as she'd slept. Those prayers had gone unanswered.

'When are you due?'

'Too soon. But right now it feels like for ever.' Her glance caught his. 'Everything is fine with the baby, if that's what you're wondering. My handing that case over has nothing to do with superstition. I just don't think I have the endurance right now for what could be a long, complicated surgery.' She pressed a hand to the small of her back. 'And if for some reason I go earlier than I expect, I don't want to pass Baby Hope over to someone else at the last second. I want it to be now, when it's a deliberate decision on both of our parts.'

That he could understand. The need to be prepared for what might happen. Unlike in his relationship with Annabelle when he'd impulsively issued an ultimatum, hoping to save her from the grief of repeating a tragic cycle—not to mention the dangerous physical symptoms she'd been experiencing.

It had worked. But not quite in the way he'd expected.

This was not where he wanted his thoughts to head. He'd do better to stick with what he could control and leave the rest of it to the side at the moment.

'Your patients will be in good hands. I'll make sure of it.'

'Thank you. That means a lot to me.' She sent him a smile that was genuine. 'Do you have any other questions before we officially end our tour and go on to discuss actual cases?'

'Just one.'

'All right.' The wariness he'd sensed during his mention of Montanari filtered back into her eyes. She had no need to be worried. He was done with discussing personal issues.

'Is the food as bad here as it was at my last gig?'

Sienna actually laughed. 'I'll let you be the judge of that. I don't mind it. But then again, I eat almost anything, as long as it isn't alive or shaped like a snake.'

'Well, on those two points we can agree. So I take it Teddy's doesn't serve exotic fare.'

'Nope. Just watery potatoes and tasteless jelly.'

He glanced at his watch and smiled back at her. 'Well, then, in the name of science, I think I should go and check out the competition. Can we save the case discussion until later?'

'Yes, I'm ready for a break as well. And you can tell me what you think once you've sampled what the canteen has to offer. Just watch out for the nurses.'

'Sorry?'

'Some of them have heard you were coming. While you're checking out the food, don't be surprised if they're checking you out.'

Would they be? He'd made it a point not to get involved with women at all since his separation. And he wasn't planning on changing that.

And what of Annabelle? She was a nurse. Had she been checking him out as well?

Of course not. But on that note, he'd better go and get something into his stomach. Before he did something stupid and went back down to the first floor to check on a very ill baby, and the protective nurse who hovered over her.

Annabelle wasn't good for his equilibrium. And she very definitely wasn't good for his objectivity. And no matter what, he had to keep that. Because if he allowed his heart to become too entangled with her as he cared for his patients, he would have trouble doing his job.

What Baby Hope and the rest of his patients needed was a doctor who could keep his emotions out of the surgical ward. No matter how hard that might prove to be.

Annabelle grabbed a tray and headed for the line of choices. She wasn't hungry. Or so she told herself. Her stomach had knotted again and again until there was almost no room in it for anything other than the big bowl of worry she'd dished up for herself that morning. Baby Hope was getting weaker. The crisis she'd had this morning proved it. If Max hadn't been there, Hope might have…

No, don't think about that. And Max had not been the only one in that room who could have saved her. Sienna would have called for the exact same treatment protocol. She'd seen the other woman in action.

Once upon a time, Annabelle had expected Max to play the role of saviour. It hadn't been fair to him. Or to her. He'd finally cracked under the pressure of it all. And so had she. At least her body had.

A few days after she'd lost her last babies, her abdomen and legs had swelled up with fluid from all of the hormones she'd been on and she'd been in pain; Max had rushed her to A&E. They'd given her an ultrasound again, thinking maybe some foetal tissue had been left behind. But what they'd found was that her ovaries had swelled to many times their normal size from harvesting the eggs.

There'd been no magic-wand treatment to

make it all go away. Her body had had to do the hard work. She'd worn support hose to keep the fluid from accumulating in her legs, and had had to sleep sitting up in a chair to make it easier to breathe as her hormone levels had gradually gone back to normal. And the look on Max's face when the doctors had told him the cause…

It had come right on the heels of him telling her that he was done trying to have babies. It had made everything that much worse. But she'd still desperately wanted children, so she'd started keeping secret recordings of her temperature. Only the more secretive she'd got over the coming weeks, the more distant he'd become. In the end, the death knell had sounded before he'd ever found that journal.

Back to food, Annabelle.

She set her tray on the metal supports running parallel to the food selections and gazed into the glass case. Baked chicken? No. Salad? No. Fruit? Yes. She picked up a clear plastic container of fruit salad and set it on her tray, pushing it a few feet further down the line. Sandwiches? Her stomach clenched in revulsion. Not at the food, but at the thought of trying to push that bread down her oesophagus.

Broccoli? Healthy, and she normally loved it, but no. She kept moving past the selection of veggies until she hit the dessert section.

Bad Annabelle. What would your mum say?

She peered back down the row, wondering if she should reverse her steps and make better choices. Except when she glanced the way she'd come, her gaze didn't fall on food. It fell on the very person she was trying to forget. Max.

And he was with Sienna. Both were holding food trays, which meant...

Oh, no! They were eating lunch too.

It's what people do. They eat. They sleep. Her throat tightened. *They move away to far-off places.*

Sienna waved to her. 'Hey, Annabelle. Hold on. Would you like to join us? We can talk about

Baby Hope, and you can help catch Max up on the case.'

It was on the tip of her tongue to say she was going to eat back in her office, but she'd just been worrying about the baby. Any light they could shed on her prognosis should outweigh any awkwardness of eating with her ex. Right?

Right.

'Sure. I'll save you a spot.' She tossed a container of yoghurt onto her plate and then a large slice of chocolate cake for good measure. Handing her personnel card to the cashier and praying she scanned it before the pair caught up with her, she threw a smile at the woman and then headed out towards the crowd of people already parked at tables.

Setting her tray on one of the only available tables in the far corner, she hesitated. Should she really be doing this?

Yes. Anything for Baby Hope.

She shut her eyes. Was she becoming as obsessed with this infant as she had been with her quest to become pregnant all those years ago?

No. Looking back now, those attempts seemed so futile. Desperate attempts by a desperate woman. Max's childhood had been pretty awful, and she'd wanted to show him how it should be. How wonderful hers had been. And since he had no blood relatives left alive, she'd wanted to give him that physical connection—for the roots she'd had with her own extended family to take hold and spread. Only none of it had worked.

If her sister hadn't had a devastating experience when trying to adopt a baby, Annabelle might have gone that route after her first miscarriage. But if the grief she'd felt after losing a baby she'd never met was horrific, how much worse had it been for her sister, who'd held a baby in her arms for months only to have to hand him back over to the courts weeks before the adoption was finalised? The whole family had been shattered. And so Annabelle had continued on her quest to have a biological child, only to fail time and time again.

She popped open the lid to her fruit, realising it was the only truly healthy thing on her plate. She'd just wanted to get out of that canteen line at any cost.

Her mouth twisted sideways. It looked as if the final cost would be paid by her waistline and hips. She shoved a huge blueberry into her mouth and bit down hard just as Max and Sienna joined her. Juice spurted over her teeth and drummed at the backs of her lips, seeking the nearest available exit.

Perfect. She covered her mouth with her napkin as she continued to fight with the food, finally swallowing it down with a couple of coughs afterwards.

Max frowned as he sat. 'Okay?'

'Yes.' Another cough, louder this time, a few people at neighbouring tables glancing her way. Probably wondering who they were going to have to do the Heimlich on this time. She swallowed again, clearing her throat. 'Just went down the wrong pipe.'

Sienna, who arrived with only some kind of green bottled concoction that made Annabelle horrified at what her own plate contained, twisted the lid to her liquid lunch and sat down. She nodded at the selection. 'I'm finding smaller portions are easier to handle when I'm working. I'll eat a proper meal when I go off duty.'

Forcing herself to cut a chunk of melon into more manageable pieces, she wished she could be just as disciplined as the surgeon. Well, today was not a good day to stand in judgement of herself. Was it any wonder she was seeking out comfort food? Her husband had just landed back in her life.

She couldn't even pretend to have a boyfriend, because if there'd been anyone serious she obviously would have wanted to pressure Max into signing the divorce papers. But she hadn't.

Ugh! She chewed quickly and then swallowed, thankful that at least this time she wasn't choking.

A phone chirped and all three of them looked down at their devices, making her smile. Her screen was blank, so it wasn't Ella, who she hadn't heard from all day, which was unusual. Maybe she hadn't heard that Max was back.

Or maybe she had.

Sienna frowned, setting her drink down on the table so quickly the contents sloshed, almost coming over the rim of the bottle. She stared at her phone for several seconds, not touching the screen. Either it was very good news...or very...

The other doctor stood up, her tongue flicking out to moisten her lips. 'I'm sorry, I have to go.' She glanced at Max. 'Can you carry on without me?'

'Of course. Is everything all right?'

'It will be.' Her hand went to her midsection. And rather than responding to whoever had sent a message, she dropped her phone into the pocket of her scrubs and picked up her drink, screwing the cap back on. 'Page me if you have any questions or need help.'

'I think I'm good.' Max sent Annabelle a wry glance. 'I'm sure Anna can answer any questions about Hope or the hospital I might have.'

Or about why he hadn't severed those final ties that bound them together?

Somehow, though, she doubted he was any more eager to revisit their past than she was. But still, the last thing she wanted today was to play hospital adviser to a man who still made her knees quake. She had no idea why that was so. She was over him. Had been for the last couple of years. In fact, she hadn't thought of him in…

Well, the last fifteen seconds, but that didn't count, since he was sitting right across from her. Before today, she'd gone weeks at a time without him crossing her mind.

But since Sienna was glancing her way as if needing reassurance that it was indeed okay to leave them alone without a referee, Annabelle nodded. 'Go. It'll be fine.'

Looking a little doubtful, but evidently not enough to want to stick around, the cardiothoracic surgeon gave a quick wave and headed towards the entrance of the canteen. Annabelle noticed she slid her phone out of her pocket and stared at the screen again as she rounded the corner.

She wondered what that was all about. But it was really none of her business.

But Baby Hope was, and since that was why Sienna had wanted to sit with her...

'Is there some news about the baby?' Maybe that was what the message was about. Could it be that...? 'Could a heart have become available?'

Hope sparked in her chest, flaring to life with a jolt that had her leaning forward and sent her plastic fork dropping back onto her tray.

Max must have seen something in her face because he shook his head. 'No. Not yet. I think she would have told us if that message had anything to do with a donor heart.'

She sagged back into her chair. 'I was hoping...'

'I know. Why don't we work on things we can control until one is available? Tell me anything else you can think of about her. The events surrounding her birth, et cetera.'

'Are you looking for something in particular?' She'd told him pretty much everything she knew back in the special care baby unit.

Max pulled a small notebook out of one of the pockets of his jacket. 'I can look at her chart and get the mechanics. But tell me about *her*. Anything out of the ordinary that you've noticed that you think might help.'

She picked up her fork and pushed around a few more blueberries, not trying to really stab any of them but using the empty gesture as a way to sort through her thoughts about Hope.

'She's a fighter. She came into this world crying as hard as her tiny lungs would let her.' She sucked down a quick breath. 'Her mother didn't even touch her. Hope was very sick and might not have survived the night, but she never asked to hold her or tried to keep us from taking her away. Maybe she already knew she was going to leave her behind and was afraid to let herself get attached.'

'You were there when she was born.'

'Yes. When the mum came in—already in labour—the doctor examined her. He didn't like the way the baby's heartbeat sounded so they did an ultrasound. They immediately saw there was a problem, so they called Sienna down.' Annabelle gripped her fork tighter. 'She knew as soon as she looked at the monitor that it was serious. So when she delivered there was a roomful of staff, just in case Hope coded on the table. They did a Caesarean section, trying to save the baby any undue stress during delivery.'

'It worked. She's still alive.'

'Yes. But she's all alone. Her mum has never even called to check on her. Not once.'

'And say what?' Max's jaw tightened. 'Maybe she didn't want to have to deal with the fallout of what might happen if it all went wrong.'

'It was her child. How could she not want to be there for her?'

'She could have felt the baby was better off without her.'

Something about the tight way he said those words made her wonder if Max was still talking about Baby Hope and her mum, or something a little closer to home.

Had he felt she was better off without him?

Rubbish. It hadn't been his idea to leave. It had been hers. If he'd truly loved her, he would have fought for her.

But Max had always had a hard time forming attachments, thanks to parents who did their utmost to avoid any show of affection. And those long trips they'd taken without him—leaving Max to wonder if they were ever coming back. If they missed him at all. Annabelle had cried when he'd told her in halting words the way things had been in his home. Her own family's open affection and need to be with each other had seemed to fascinate him.

Maybe he really could understand how a mum could abandon her own child. In many ways, Max had felt abandoned. Maybe even by her, when she'd told him to leave.

She should have just given up when he'd given her that last ultimatum. But she hadn't—she'd wanted Max to have what his parents had denied him. And when he'd found her journal… God, he'd been so furious that night. To forestall any more arguments, she'd told him to get out. The memories created a sour taste in her mouth.

'I guess I'll never know what her true motivation was for leaving. If I had, maybe I could have changed her mind, or at least talked her into coming back to check on Hope.'

'She probably wouldn't have. Come back, that is. Maybe she felt that once she walked out, there was no going back.'

This time when his eyes came up to meet hers there was no denying that he was talking about something other than their patient.

Unable to come up with anything that wouldn't

inflame the situation further, she settled for a shrug. 'Maybe not. I guess people just have to learn to live with the consequences of their choices.'

As Annabelle had had to do.

And with that statement, she made the choice to stab her fork into the slab of chocolate cake on her plate and did her best to steer the conversation back to neutral territory. Where there was no chance of loaded statements or examining past regrets too closely.

But even as they spoke of the hospital and its patients and advances in treatment, she was very aware that nothing could ever be completely neutral as far as Max went.

So she would try to do as she'd stated and make the very best choices she could while he was here. And then learn to live with the consequences.

CHAPTER THREE

'ELLA, LET'S NOT have this discussion right now.'

'What discussion is that?' Her best friend batted her eyes, while Annabelle's rolled around in their sockets. 'The prodigal returns to the scene of his crime?'

'That doesn't even make any sense.'

'It doesn't have to. So spill. I haven't seen you since I heard the big news. Not from you, I might add. What's up with that?'

She tried to delay the inevitable. 'What news are you talking about?'

Ella made a scoffing sound as she leaned against the exam table. 'That a certain ex has crashed back onto the scene.'

Crashed was a very good word for what he'd done. 'There's nothing to tell. He showed up yesterday at the hospital.'

'Out of the blue? With no advance notice?' Her friend lifted the bottle of water she held, taking a quick drink. She then grimaced.

'Are you okay?'

'Fine. Just a little tummy trouble. I hope I'm not coming down with whatever everyone else has. Wouldn't that be a wonderful Christmas present?' She twisted her lips and then shrugged. 'Anyway, you had no idea he was coming?'

'Of course not. I would have told you, if I'd known.' And probably caught the next available flight out of town. Annabelle sighed, already tired of this line of questioning. When had life become so complicated? 'I'm sure someone knew he was coming. I just never thought to ask because I never dreamed...'

'That Max Ainsley would show up on your doorstep and beg for your forgiveness?'

'Ella!' Annabelle hurried over to the door to the exam room and shut it before anyone overheard their conversation. She turned back to face her friend. 'First of all, he did not show up on my doorstep. He just happened to come to work at the hospital. I'm sure he had no idea I was working here any more than I knew that he was the one taking Sienna's place. And second, there's no need for him to apologise.'

'Like hell there's not. He practically abandoned you without a word.'

Oh, Lord, she'd had very little sleep last night and now this. As soon as she'd finished lunch with Max yesterday, she had got out of that canteen as fast as she possibly could. Even so, he'd come down to the special care baby unit a couple of hours later to get even more information on Baby Hope. Clinical information this time about blood types and the matching tests they'd done in the hope that a heart would become available.

She'd been forced to stand there as he shuffled through papers and tried to absorb any tiny piece of information that could help with the newborn's treatment. With his head bent over the computer screen, each little shift in his expression had triggered memories of happier times. Which was why she'd lain in bed and tossed and turned for hours last night. Because she couldn't help but dissect the whole day time and time again.

Sheer exhaustion had finally pulled her under just as the sun had begun to rise. And then she'd had to get up and come into work, knowing she was going to run into him again today. And tomorrow. And three months from now.

How was she going to survive until his contract ended?

'He didn't abandon me. It simply didn't work out between us. We both had a part in ending it, even though I asked him to leave.'

It was true. She couldn't see it back then, and Ella had had to listen to her long-distance calls as she'd cycled through the stages of grief, giving sympathy where it was needed and a proverbial kick in the backside when she was still wearing her heart on her sleeve six months after the separation.

'Enough!' she'd finally declared. 'You have to decide whether you want to start your life over again or if you're going to spend it crying over a man who isn't coming back.'

Those words had done what nothing else had been able to. They'd convinced her that she needed to climb out of the pity pit she'd dug for herself and start giving back to society. What better way to forget about your own heartache than to ease the suffering of someone else?

Ella had talked her into moving from London to the Cotswolds soon afterwards. It had been one of the best decisions of her life.

Well. Until now. But that hadn't been Ella's fault. It had been no one's. Not even Max's.

Annabelle's pager suddenly beeped at the same time as Ella's, and they both jumped at the noise. Peering down to look at what had caused the alert, Annabelle read.

A multi-vehicle accident on the M5 has occurred. A hired bus for a nursery school outing was involved. Several of those patients

*are en route—eta five minutes. All available
personnel please report to A&E.*

'Oh, God,' she said, reaching for her friend's
hand.

'I know. Let's head over.' Her friend stopped
and gripped the edge of the table for a second.

'Ella?'

'I'm okay.' She ran a hand through her hair,
her face pale. 'Let's go.'

'Maybe you should go home instead.' Almost
a third of the hospital staff was out due to a
virus that had spread through their ranks. Hopefully Ella wasn't the latest person to fall victim
to the bug.

Her friend blew out a breath. 'I hope to God
I'm not...' She stopped again. 'I'll be all right.
If I start feeling worse, I'll go home, okay?'

'Are you sure?'

'Yes. Now, let's get our butts in gear and go
and help whoever is coming.'

Max spotted her the second she came out of
the lift. She and a familiar redhead hurried past

a small Christmas tree towards the assembled staff who were waiting for the first of the ambulances to arrive. The other woman sent him a chilling glare. Perfect. It was Ella. She'd always had it in for him.

It didn't matter.

His ex moved over to him. 'Any word yet?'

'I don't know any more than you do.'

Just then, he caught the sound of a siren in the distance. And then another. Once they hit, they would have to do triage—the kind he'd done during his stints with Doctors Without Borders. This hospital might be more modern than the ones he'd worked in over the last six months, but that didn't mean that the process of sorting patients from most critical to least would be any easier. Especially not when it came to those involving high-speed crashes. He had to be ready for anything, including cardiac involvement from chest trauma.

He'd never got used to the cries of suffering while he was in Africa. And it would be no easier here than it had been there.

A nursery school outing! Of all things.

Right now, they didn't even know exactly how many patients were coming in, much less the seriousness of the injuries.

Then the first emergency vehicle spun into the space in front of the hospital, another stopping right behind it. And, yes, the screams of a child as those back doors were opened cut through him like a knife.

He moved in to look as the stretcher rolled backwards and onto the ground. A child who couldn't be more than three came into view, blood covering the sheet of the stretcher. And her right arm… Her shirt sleeve had been cut and parted to reveal the raw flesh of an open fracture, the pearly edge of a bone peeking through.

One of the orthopaedists moved in. 'Take her to exam room one. Take vitals, check her for other injuries. I'll be there in a minute.' He knew that doctors hated assigning priorities to treatment, but it was the only way to save as many lives as possible. If they treated these patients according to the order they came in, they might condemn a more seriously injured patient to death. It couldn't work that way. Max knew that from experience.

A nurse directed the paramedic back towards the interior of the hospital where other staff were preparing to receive whoever came through those doors.

The assembled doctors met each stretcher as it arrived, specialists matched up with the appropriate accident victims. When Annabelle tried to follow one of the other doctors, Max stopped her. If a critical case came his way, he would need a nurse to assist. And who better than a nurse who dealt with crises on a daily basis? He'd seen her in action when Baby Hope's pulse ox levels had plummeted. She'd been calm and confident, exactly what he needed.

It wasn't an unreasonable request.

And it had nothing to do with their past, or the fact that working with someone he knew would be easier than a complete stranger. He already knew that he and Annabelle made a great team on a professional level. They'd worked together many times before, since they'd been employed by the same hospital in London during their marriage.

The next ambulance pulled into the bay. The driver leaped out just as the doors at the back of the vehicle swung open.

'How many more are coming?' Max called. So far they'd had thirteen patients ranging in age from two to four years in addition to three nursery school workers who'd also sustained injuries. The rescue in the frigid November temperatures had taken its toll as well. Despite being wrapped in blankets, many of the patients were shivering from shock and exposure.

'This is the last one. She was trapped between seats. She sustained blunt force trauma to the chest. She threw PVCs the whole way over.'

When the wheels of the stretcher hit the ground and made the turn towards them, Max caught sight of a pale face and blue-tinged lips, despite the oxygen mask over her face. A little girl. Probably two years old. Disposable electrode pads had been adhered to a chest that heaved as she gasped for breath.

'How bad?'

The paramedic shook his head. 'Difficulty breathing, pulse ox low as is her BP. And her EKG readings are all over the chart. PVCs, a couple of quick ventricular arrhythmias, but nothing sustained.'

'Possible cardiac contusion. Let's get her inside.'

As soon as they ran through the doors, Max glanced at her. 'We're going straight to ICU. You'll have to tell me where to go.'

With Annabelle calling out instructions they arrived on the third-floor unit within minutes. The paramedic had stayed with them the whole time, assisting with moving the stretcher.

They burst through the entrance to the unit, and Max grabbed every staff member who wasn't already treating someone and motioned them to the nearest empty room. Together they worked to get the girl hooked up to a heart monitor and take her vitals. The child was conscious, her wide eyes were open, and, although there were tears trickling from the corners of her eyes, her struggle to breathe took precedence over crying.

Somehow that just made it worse.

'We need to intubate, and then I want to get some X-rays and a CAT scan.'

He was hearing some crepitus as she breathed, the popping and crackling sounds as her chest expanded indicative of a possible sternal fracture. It could also explain some of her cardiac symptoms. The faster he figured it out, the better the prognosis.

He leaned down to the child, wishing he at least knew her name. 'We're going to take good care of you.'

Within minutes they'd slid a trach tube into place to regulate her breathing. Her cardiac function was still showing some instability, but it hadn't worsened. At least not yet.

Max was a master of remaining objective during very difficult surgeries. But there was something about children who were victims of accidents that threatened to shred his composure. These weren't neat put-the-child-to-sleep-in-a-controlled-setting cases. These were painful, awful situations that wrung him out emotionally.

Needing to come home from the Sudan to maintain his certification couldn't have come at a better time. He'd desperately needed a rest; the abject poverty and suffering he'd seen had taken their toll on him.

And yet here he was, his second day on the job, feeling as if he'd been thrown right back onto the front lines.

Mentally and emotionally.

Annabelle helped him get the girl ready to move to the radiology section, glancing at him as she did. She touched the youngster every chance she got, probably as a way to reassure her. He'd noticed her doing the same thing with Baby Hope.

Those tiny gestures of compassion struck at something deep inside him.

Strands of hair stuck to a face moist with perspiration, and yet Annabelle was totally oblivious to everything except her patient.

Just then, as if she sensed him looking at her, her head came up. Their gazes tangled for several long seconds. Then they were right back at it. Annabelle was evidently willing to set any animosity aside for the benefit of their young patient.

The CT scan confirmed his suspicion. The force of the little girl striking the seat in front of her had fractured her sternum, putting pressure on her heart and lungs. A half-hour turned into an hour, which turned into five as they continued to work the case.

It had to be way past time for Annabelle's shift to end, but she didn't flinch as they struggled to stabilise the girl.

Sarah. He'd finally learned her name. And un-like Baby Hope's mum, or even his own par-ents—who'd been more angry than concerned when he'd been injured in a bike crash—Sarah's mum and dad were frantic, desperate for any shred of news.

Annabelle came in from her fifth trip to see them. 'I told them they could come see her in a few minutes.'

'Good.' Sarah was already more comfortable. They'd given her some pain medication, and al-though she was still on a ventilator they'd be able to wean her off in the next day or two, depend-ing on how much more swelling she had. 'Why don't you take a break? Get off your feet for a few minutes.'

'Sarah needs me. I'll rest when she does.'

'Have you eaten today?'

This time she smiled, although the edges of her mouth were lined with exhaustion as she re-peated the same thought. 'I'll eat when you do.'

If she thought he was calling her weak, she

was wrong. She was anything but. Of course, he already knew that. He'd watched Annabelle go to hell and back in her effort to have a child. She was as stubborn as they came. It was one of the things he'd loved most about her, and yet it was ultimately that very thing that had driven them apart.

'Is that a dinner invitation?' He cocked a brow at her.

Her smile faded. 'Of course not. I just meant—'

'I know what you meant.' His jaw stiffened. 'I was joking.'

'Of course.' Annabelle began collecting some of the discarded treatment items, not looking at him. It was then he realised how harsh his voice had been. It reminded him of the time he'd finally had enough of the procedures and the heartache. He'd been harsh then too. Very harsh, if he looked back on it now.

Max moved in closer, lifting a hand to touch her arm, then deciding better of it.

'I'm sorry for snapping at you. I would say

chalk it up to exhaustion, but that's no excuse.' He could envision this scene repeating itself ad nauseam unless he put a stop to it. 'Maybe we really should grab a bite when we're done here. We can figure out how we're going to work together for the next several months without constantly being at each other's throats.'

She glanced up at him. 'I think we can manage to bump into each other now and then without having a meltdown.'

This time the sharpness was on her side.

'I know we can.' He took a deep breath and dragged a hand through his hair. 'Look, I'm trying to figure out how to make this easier on both of us, since I assume neither one of us is going to resign.'

It wasn't just because of his contract. He'd known for a long time that this day was coming. When he'd have to face his past and decide how to move forward. Maybe that time was now. He could go on putting it off, as he had over the past three years, but this wasn't Africa where he could just immerse himself in work and not have to see her day after day. They were looking at months of working together. At least.

'I love my post.' The sharpness in her voice had given way to a slight tremor. Did she think he was going to cause trouble for her or ask her to leave?

'I know you do. And I don't want to make you miserable by being here.' This time, he touched her gloved hand. Just for a second. 'Will it really be so very hard, Anna?'

'No. It's just that I never expected to...'

'You never expected to see me again.'

'No. Honestly I didn't.'

'But we both knew we would eventually have to finalise things. We can't live in limbo for ever.' This wasn't the direction he'd wanted to go with this discussion. But now that he was here, he had to see it through.

'You're right.' She glanced down at the items in her hand and then went over to throw them in the rubbish bin. Then she moved over to the exam table and pushed the little girl's hair out of her face. The tenderness in her eyes made his stomach contract. She would have made such a wonderful mum. It was a shame that biology—and fate—kept her from being one. No power known to medical science had seemed able to work out what the problem was. Or how to fix it.

What he hadn't expected was for her to shove him out of her life the second she realised he was serious about not trying again. That bitter pill had taken ages to go down. But it finally had. And when it did, he realised his parents had taught him a valuable lesson. Keeping his heart to himself really was the better way.

When she looked up at him again, all hints of tenderness were gone, replaced by a resolute determination. 'You're right. We can't live in limbo. So this time the invitation is real. If you don't have plans, I think we should have dinner. And decide where to go from here.'

Suddenly that discussion didn't look quite as attractive as it had moments earlier. But since he'd been the one to suggest sitting down and talking things over, he couldn't very well refuse. 'Okay, once Sarah's parents have had their visit, we'll head out.'

A half-hour later, Max had scrawled the last of his instructions in Sarah's chart and set it in the holder outside her door. The girl's parents were still sitting by her bedside. He'd sent Annabelle on ahead to get her things.

As he stretched his back a couple of verte-brae popped, relieving the tension that had been building along his spine. He was dog tired. Maybe having dinner with Annabelle wasn't such a good idea. The discussion should prob-ably wait until they were both rested.

Except there'd never seemed to *be* a right time to approach their unfinished business. So they had to make time.

He went to the men's changing room and washed his hands and then bent down to splash his face. Blotting it dry with a paper towel from the dispenser, he caught a glance at his reflection.

Dark hair, still cut short from his time overseas, was just starting to grey at the temples. Where had the years gone?

One minute he'd been a happily married man, and the next he'd been on the brink of divorce and living like a nomad, going from place to place but never really settling down. Maybe he should have joined the military. Except he hadn't wanted to give up the possibility of coming back to work in his field, and he would have either had to retrain for his speciality or settled for a position as a general surgeon. He loved paediatric cardiology in a way he couldn't explain to anyone but himself. So he'd gone with Doctors Without Borders.

Only his travels had simply delayed the inevitable. He still had to face the ghosts of his past.

He didn't want to hurt Annabelle. And he wasn't quite sure why he'd never signed the papers the second he'd realised what the packet of documents contained. Maybe he'd used them as a cautionary tale of what could happen when you opened your heart up to someone. Or maybe marriage had been an easy excuse for not getting involved with anyone else—not that he ever planned on it. Some day, though, Annabelle would meet Mr. Right and would want to be free to be with him. Their old life would stand in the way of that.

So, were they going to discuss their past tonight? Or discuss how to work together in the future?

He wasn't sure. They were both tired. And probably overly emotional.

Maybe he should just let Annabelle take the lead as far as topics went. And if she decided she wanted those divorce papers signed post haste, he might just have to tackle a tough conversation after all.

CHAPTER FOUR

THE PUB WAS PACKED. And with the clanging
of plates and raucous laughter, it was hard to
think, much less carry on a civilised conversation. Not the kind of place to go after dealing
with a twelve-hour day of work.

But the place was also dark, with just some
dim wall sconces lighting the way towards the
tables. A few coloured bulbs along the bar were
the only concession to the upcoming Christmas
season.

O'Malley's wasn't a normal hospital hangout,
but that was okay. She wanted privacy. Which
was one of the reasons Annabelle had suggested
it. If they were going to have The Talk, opening up the subject of their past, she didn't want
anyone to overhear the conversation.

And the low lighting would keep Max from seeing her expression. In the past, he'd always been able to read her like a book. It had been no different in that treatment room an hour earlier, when he'd known instantly that he'd hurt her with his words and apologised. She hated that he could still decipher her expressions. And when he'd touched her...

No doubt he'd seen the heat that washed into her face. Well, this time she was going to make it a little harder on him, if she could.

They followed the waitress to a small table for two in the very back of the place. Max waited for her to sit down before pulling his own chair out.

The server plonked a menu down in front of each of them, having to speak loudly to be heard above the din. 'What would you like to drink?'

Annabelle tried to decide if she wanted to risk imbibing or if she should play it safe. Oh, what the hell? Maybe she should dull her senses just a little. 'I'll have white wine.'

Writing her request down in a little book, the

woman then turned her attention to Max. And 'turned her attention' was evidently synonymous with turning on her charm. Because suddenly the waitress was all smiles, fiddling with her hair. 'And you, sir?'

'I'll have a whisky sour, thank you.' He sent her a quick smile, but to his credit there was nothing behind it that hinted of any interest in whatever the waitress was offering. And she was offering. As a woman, Annabelle recognised the signs, even though she had never gone the flirting route.

At least not until she met Max.

Evidently realising she was out of luck, the woman shifted her gaze to Max's left hand, then she snapped her little book shut and flounced off.

Max didn't wear his ring any more. But then again, neither did she.

'Thank you for that.'

Max tilted his head. 'For what?'

'Not responding to her in front of me.'

Up went one brow. 'Not my type.'

That made her laugh, and her muscles all loosened. 'Really? Because she seemed to think you were hers.'

'I hadn't noticed.'

'Oh, come on.' She sat back in her chair and studied him. Max had always been handsome. But in the three years since she'd seen him, he'd grown even more attractive, although there was a deep groove between his brows that she didn't remember seeing when they were together.

'Seriously. She was probably just being friendly.'

'Seriously, huh? I don't know. Maybe we should make a little bet on it.'

'I don't bet on things like that.' The furrow above his nose deepened. 'Not any more.'

He didn't bet on what? Relationships? Because of her?

That wasn't what she wanted for Max. His childhood had been rough as it was, devoid of affection…love. He deserved to be happy, and she wanted that for him. Even now.

'We never really talked about it. What happened all those years ago.' Suddenly she wished she'd chosen a place a little less loud as she fingered the plastic placemat in front of her.

'I seem to remember a *lot* of talking. Most of it angry.'

Yes, there had been the arguments. Especially at the end, when he'd found her journal, the smoking gun that she was still hoping against hope that she would become pregnant.

Even before that, though, Max had become someone she didn't recognise. Impatient. Short. And somehow sad. That was the worst of all the emotions she'd seen in him. She'd tried so hard to have a child, thinking it would make everything better between them. That it would bind Max to her in a physical way—give him a sense of roots. Instead, it had only made things worse. The pregnancy attempts had ended up becoming a vicious cycle of failure and then increased desperation. Instead of binding them together, her attempts had torn them apart.

The waitress came and set their drinks in front of them. 'Are you ready to order?' Her voice wasn't nearly as friendly this time.

'Fish and chips for me and a glass of water, please.' Annabelle was craving good, old-fashioned fare.

'I'll have the same. And a dark ale to go with it, please.'

Annabelle didn't remember Max being a big drinker. Not that two drinks constituted an alcoholic. He just seemed…harder, somehow. Less approachable. Like his parents?

Once the waitress was gone, Annabelle picked up her wine, sipping with care.

Max, however, lifted his own glass and took a deep drink. 'I haven't had one of these in a long time. This place was a good choice.'

'Ella and I like to come here every once in a while. It's out of the way and loud enough that you don't have to think.'

He seemed to digest that for a moment. 'Not as loud as some of the places I've been.'

Interesting.

'Where *have* you been? If you don't mind my asking.' She didn't feel like talking about the arguments or failures of the past.

'I don't. I joined up with Doctors Without Borders. In between contracts in England, I've gone wherever they've needed me. Kenya, a time or two, but mostly the Sudan. I spent the last six months there.'

Annabelle listened, fascinated, as he shared what he'd done in the years since he'd left their flat. Some of the stories were horrifying. 'Isn't it hard to see that?'

'Yes.'

'And yet you keep going back. After this contract is up and Sienna is back from maternity leave, will you return there?'

The waitress arrived with their food and drinks, quickly asking if they needed anything else.

'I think we're good, thank you.'

When they were alone again, he drank the last of his whisky. 'I don't know what I'm going to do once this contract is up. I've been thinking about settling someplace on a more permanent basis.'

From what he'd told her, he'd hopped from city to city, country to country as the whim took him.

She was on her first bite of fish when he asked, 'How long have you lived in Cheltenham?'

It took her a second to chew and swallow. 'A year. I went to live with my mum for a while after…well, after you left.'

'Suzanne told me you didn't stay in the flat for long.'

Annabelle had missed their cleaning lady. 'Did you think I would?'

'I didn't really know what you would do. I went back after my first trip, almost a year later, and you were gone.'

'I just couldn't…stay.'

'Neither could I.' He paused. 'Even if you

hadn't asked me to go, I would have. Things were never going to change.'

This was the most she'd ever been able to drag out of him. And she wasn't even having to drag. Back then they would fight, and then Max would clam up for days on end, his tight jaw attesting to the fact that he was holding his emotions at bay with difficulty.

He'd once told her that his parents had been the same way with him—their anger had translated into silence. He'd struggled with breaking those old patterns their entire marriage. But in the last six months of it, those habits had come back with a vengeance. If she'd tried to probe or make things right between them—with the offer of physical intimacy—he'd always seemed to have some meeting or suddenly had a shift at the hospital. She'd finally got the message: he didn't want to be with her, except when absolutely necessary for the in-vitro procedures. And then, after her last miscarriage, he was done trying for a baby.

Actually, Max had been done. Full stop. He'd left their relationship long before he'd actually walked out of the door.

She took another sip of her water to moisten her mouth as she got ready to tackle the most difficult subject of all.

'You haven't signed the papers.'

There was a pause.

'No. I've been overseas on and off.' He shrugged. 'After a while, I forgot about them.'

That stung, but she tried not to let it. 'Doesn't it make going out on dates awkward?'

'I've been busy. No time—or inclination—to jump back into those waters.'

His answer made Annabelle cringe. 'I'm sorry if I'm the reason for that.'

'I just haven't seen many happy marriages.'

'My parents are happy.'

He smiled at that. 'They are the exception to the rule. How are they?'

'They're fine. So are my sisters. Jessica had another boy while you were gone—his name is

Nate.' She didn't want to delve into the fact that her parents' and siblings' relationships had all seemed to work out just swimmingly. Except for hers.

'That's wonderful. I'm happy for them.'

Popping a chip into her mouth, she tried not to think about how different their childhoods had been. Max's parents had seemed unhappy to be tied down with a child. They'd evidently loved to travel, and he had cramped their style.

Annabelle's home, on the other hand, had been filled with love and laughter, and when her parents had travelled—on long road trips, mostly—their kids had gone with them. She had wonderful memories of those adventures.

She'd hoped she and Max could have the same type of relationship. Instead, she'd become so focused on a single aspect of what constituted a family that she'd ignored the other parts.

Had she been so needy back then that she'd damaged Max somehow?

Well, hadn't their breakup damaged her?

Yes, but not in the way she'd expected. Annabelle had grown thicker skin over the past three years. Before, it seemed as if her whole life had been about Max and their quest to have a family. When that had begun breaking down and she'd sensed a lack of support on Max's side to continue, she'd become more and more withdrawn. She could see now how she'd withheld love whenever Max hadn't done exactly what she'd wanted. Just as his parents had.

She regretted that more than anything.

'So what do you want to do about it?'

He set his glass down. 'About what?'

Did she need to spell it out? 'About the paperwork. Maybe this is the reason we've been thrown back together. To tie up loose ends.'

A smile tilted up one side of his mouth. 'So I'm a loose end, now, am I?'

Nothing about Max was loose. He'd always been lean and fit, but now there was a firmness to him that spoke of muscle. Like the biceps that just peeked out from beneath the polo shirt he'd changed into before leaving the hospital.

They'd checked on Baby Hope before taking off. She was still holding her own, against all odds. But if a donor heart was not found soon...

She shrugged off the thought. 'You're not a loose end. But maybe I'm one of yours. You could be happy, Max. Find the right woman, and—'

'You're not a loose end, either.' His hand covered hers, an index finger coaxing hers to curl around it. The sensation was unbearably intimate and so like times past that she was helpless not to respond to the request. Their fingers twined. Tightened. The same heat from the exam room sloshed up her neck and into her face.

'Are you done with your meal?'

Her eyes widened. 'Yes. Why?'

'Would you mind coming with me for a minute?' He threw some notes onto the table, and, without even waiting for the bill, got to his feet.

She swallowed hard, wondering if he'd had

enough of this conversation. Maybe he even had his signed divorce papers back in his office. If so, she hoped she wouldn't burst into tears when he presented her with them.

But he'd just told her she wasn't a loose end. And he'd held her hand in a way that had been so familiar it had sent a sting of fear through her heart.

So she picked up her coat and followed him through the pub, weaving through tables and people alike. When their waitress made to stop them, Max murmured something to her. She nodded and disappeared back among the tables of customers.

At the door, Max helped her into her coat and they went out into the dark night. It was chilly, but it wasn't actually as cold as she expected. When Max kept on walking, rather than stopping to let her know why they'd left the restaurant, she remained by his side. She had no idea where they were going, but right now she didn't care.

A taxi stopped at the kerb. 'You looking for a fare?'

'I think we're okay.' Max glanced at her as if to confirm his words. She gave a quick nod, and the cab driver pulled away in search of another customer. The bar was probably a perfect spot to do that, actually, since anyone who'd had a few too many drinks would need a way to get safely back to their flat. Putting her hands in her pockets, she waited for him to tell her why he'd brought her out here. Maybe something was wrong with him physically. Could that be why he'd come home from the Sudan?

A few minutes later, she couldn't take not knowing. 'Is everything okay?'

'It's still there, isn't it, despite everything?'

She frowned, moving under one of the street lamps along the edge of a park. 'What is?'

'That old spark.'

She'd felt that spark the second she'd laid eyes on him all those years ago. But he wasn't talking about way back then. He was talking about right now.

'Yes,' she whispered.

She wished to hell it weren't. But she wasn't going to pay truth back with a lie.

'Anna…' He took her hand and eased them off the path and into the dark shadows of a nearby bench.

She sat down, before she fell down. His voice… She would recognise that tone anywhere. He sat beside her, still holding her hand.

'You've changed,' he said.

'So have you. You seem…' She shook her head, unable to put words to her earlier thoughts. Or maybe it was that she wasn't sure she should.

'That bad, huh?'

'No. Not at all.'

He grinned, the flash of his teeth sending a shiver over her. 'That good, then, huh?'

Annabelle laughed and nudged him with her shoulder. 'You wish.'

'I actually do.'

When his fingers shifted from her hand to just beneath her chin, the shiver turned to a whoosh as all the breath left her body, her nerve endings suddenly attuned to Max's every move. And when his head came down, all she felt was anticipation.

Max wasn't sure what had come over him or made him want to leave the safety of the bar, but the second his lips touched hers all bets were off. The fragrance of her shampoo mixed with the normal sterile hospital scents, and it was like coming home after a long hard day.

His fingers slid up her jawline, edged behind the feminine curve of her ear and tunnelled into her hair. Annabelle's body shifted as well, turning into him, her arms winding around his neck in a way he hadn't felt in far too long. Or with any other woman.

The truth was that simple. And that complicated. No woman would ever be able to take Anna's place—so he'd never even tried to find one.

He deepened the kiss, tongue touching her lips, exulting in the fact that she opened to him immediately. No hesitation.

They'd always been good in bed, each instinctively knowing what the other wanted and each had been more than willing to oblige. Soft and sweet or daring and adventurous, Anna had always been open to trying new things. Until it had become all about...

No. No thinking about that right now.

Not when she was clutching the lapels of his jacket as if she could tug him into her very soul.

He angled his head, thrusting a little deeper into the heat of her mouth. Maybe they should just forget about the cold park and head back to the warmth of his cottage and the heat they'd find in his bed. There were taxis on practically every corner.

That was what he wanted: to have her. In bed. Skin to skin. With nothing between them but fire and raw need.

Just as he was getting ready to edge back

enough to ask her to go with him, the sound of voices broke through the haze of passion.

Not Anna's voice, but someone else's. Close enough that he could tell they were man and woman.

Annabelle beat him to the punch, pulling back so suddenly that it left him reeling for a few seconds. She glanced at him and he looked back at her. They both smiled. Young medical students caught necking. It had happened before, when they'd been dating. Only that had been a police officer, who'd not been quite as amused by their antics.

'Caught again,' he murmured.

'So it would seem.'

He looked over to see who was walking past and his smile died, icy fingers walking up his spine. It was indeed a man and a woman, but they were pushing a pram. Bundles and bundles of blankets were piled on top of what had to be a young infant. And their faces.

God. They were happy. Incredibly happy.

His gaze went back to Anna's to find that all colour had drained from her skin, leaving her pasty white. The young man threw them a smile and a quick hello.

Somehow Max managed to croak something back, but the mood was spoiled. He could tell by Anna's reaction that she'd been thrown back to the tragedy that had been their shared past. At least that was what he took her stricken gaze to mean—the way her hungry eyes followed that pram as it went past and disappeared into the darkness.

His teeth gritted together several times before he had the strength to stand up and say what needed to be said. 'I think we've both had a little too much to drink. Maybe it's time to call it a night.'

Anna's one glass of wine and his two weightier beverages did not constitute drunkenness by any stretch of the imagination. Unless you considered being drunk on memories of the past as over-imbibing. It had to be all the reminiscing they'd done in the restaurant and the way her face had softened as she'd looked across the table at him. He'd always had trouble resisting her, and tonight was no exception. After one smile, he'd been putty in her hands. But he'd better somehow figure out how to put a stop to whatever was happening between them before one of them got hurt.

He'd opened his heart to her once before only to have it diced into tiny pieces and handed back to him. Never again. He would do whatever it took to keep that stony organ locked in the vault of his chest.

Far out of reach of her or anyone else.

CHAPTER FIVE

'I JUST HEARD. There's a heart. Get to the hospital.'

It took several seconds before a still-groggy Annabelle realised who was on the phone and what he was talking about. Once she did, she leaped to her feet, glancing at the clock on her nightstand to see what time it was. Three a.m.

Once a donor organ was located time was of the essence. It had to be transplanted within hours. 'I'm on my way.'

Scurrying around as fast as she could, she found clothes and shoved her limbs into them, not worrying about how she looked other than a quick brush of her teeth and putting her hair up into a high ponytail. Then she was out of the door and on her way to Teddy's. It was pitch black as she pulled her car out onto the roadway, and there were almost no other vehicles out this late. Blinking the remaining sleep from her eyes, she thought about the tasks she needed to do once she arrived.

Max evidently wasn't at the hospital yet, since he'd said he'd just heard. Which meant they'd tracked him down at home. Wherever that was.

Last night after that disastrous kiss, he'd seen her home in a taxi, before giving her a tight wave as the driver pulled away. What had she been thinking letting him kiss her?

Letting him? More like her yanking him to her as tightly as she could. Once his lips had made contact with hers, he'd have been hard pressed to get away from her. She'd been that desperate to have him keep kissing her on into eternity.

Only that hadn't happened.

She tightened her grip on the steering wheel. No, that couple with the baby had walked by ruining everything. It hadn't been their fault, nor could they have known that Max's face had hardened instantly, reverting back to the mask she remembered from the end of their marriage. Was he remembering how badly he'd wanted what she couldn't deliver? No, he'd told her he no longer wanted children—maybe he didn't want to see reminders of what could have been.

And the way he'd looked at her after the young couple had walked away...

As if he couldn't wait to get away from her. He'd pulled her up from that bench so fast her head had spun. And no mention of when they would see each other again.

They wouldn't, obviously. Not outside the hospital. Or outside surgical suites. Last night had been a mistake. A remnant of embers long since extinguished. Except for one tiny spark...

Wasn't that what he'd called it? A spark?

Why had he even called her about the heart? He could have operated on Hope in the middle of the night, and she would have known nothing about it until the next morning. Had he been worried about how upset she would be that he hadn't told her?

Or was it simply the courtesy of a doctor to another member of a patient's medical team?

That was probably it.

Well, it didn't do any good to think about it now. This call was what Annabelle had been waiting for during the past two weeks. News that this particular baby might have a chance to live and grow.

She could put aside any discomfort working beside Max might bring. He and Sienna were both top in their field. She halfway wondered if the other doctor would be performing the transplant surgery. But Sienna had turned the case over to Max. Which meant he would be doing it.

Would he let her in the operating room? She wasn't a surgical nurse, but she had done a rotation in the surgical suite. And she wanted to be there for Hope, even though the baby would have no idea she was there. And wouldn't care.

She reached the hospital and made her way to the staff car park area. From the looks of the empty spaces, people still hadn't recovered from the virus. Hopefully Max would be able to find enough healthy bodies to be able to perform the surgery in the middle of the night. Well, by the time things were all prepped, it would probably be closer to six o'clock in the morning. Still early, but not so far out that it would be hard to talk people into coming in to assist.

Hurrying to the main entrance, she was surprised to find Max waiting for her. 'I thought you'd be in prepping for surgery.'

'We're still waiting on the medevac to get here with the heart.'

She walked with him, his long steps eating the distance. 'Do you know anything about it?'

'It typed right for Hope. The donor was an infant…the victim of a drunk driver. The family signed off just a few hours ago.'

Signed off. Such an impersonal term for what was a very personal decision. That baby had been someone's pride and joy. Their life. She'd mourned the foetuses she'd miscarried. But how much more would she ache if she'd held those children in her arms only to have them taken away by a cruel set of circumstances?

Kind of like the devastation her sister had experienced when she'd tried to adopt. But at least that child was still alive somewhere in the world.

A telltale prickle behind her eyelids warned her to move her thoughts to something else. Like the way Max had sounded saying Baby Hope's name.

Max had always been good at making sure parents knew that he thought of his tiny patients as people, painstakingly remembering even the names of extended family members. It was one of the things she'd truly loved about him. How special he made people feel.

It was what had drawn her to him when they'd first met. He'd acted as if she were the most beautiful girl in the room. Well, Max had certainly been the best-looking guy she'd ever laid eyes on, and when he'd said her name it had made her—

'Anna? You okay?'

She scrubbed her eyes with her palms. 'Still fighting the last bits of sleep, but I'll be fine.'

It was a lie. Annabelle was wide awake, but she was not going to tell him that she'd been standing there remembering the way they'd once been together.

'Well, you'd better finish waking up. We have a lot of work to do before that heart arrives.'

'Were you able to assemble a transplant team?'

He nodded, looking sideways at her as they continued down the brightly painted corridor. Annabelle had always loved the way Teddy's was so cheerful, almost as if it were a wonderful place for kids to laugh and play rather than a hospital that treated some of the most desperately ill children in the area.

'You're part of that team.'

Annabelle stopped in her tracks. She'd hoped he would include her in some way, but to put her on the actual team… That strange prickling sensation grew stronger. 'Are you serious?'

'I wouldn't have said it if I weren't.'

'Thank you. You don't know what this means to me.'

'I think I do.' He smiled, no hint of awkwardness in his manner, unlike Annabelle, who could barely look at him without remembering what had happened last night. 'But I didn't put you on it out of some sense of pity. I need you. You know Hope better than probably anyone else here at the hospital. I want you monitoring her, letting me know of anything out of the ordinary you see as we get her ready. And I want a sense of how she is when the surgery is finished, and she's coming out of the anaesthetic.'

More beautiful words had never been spoken. Max acted as if it were a given that the baby would survive the surgery and actually wake up on the other side. As if there were no question about it. Done for her sake? Or because he really believed it? 'You've probably studied her case as much as I have.'

'I've studied it, but you've lived it, Anna.'

She *had* lived it. Some of it joyful, like when

Hope opened those sweet blue eyes of hers and stared into Annabelle's. Some of them terrifying...like the day before yesterday when she had gone into respiratory failure. Annabelle had thought for sure those were the last moments of the baby's life. And now this. The sweet sound of hope...for a precious baby who was fighting so hard to live.

And now she just might get that chance.

'Thank you. For letting me be a part of it.'

Max started moving again, his steps quicker, more confident. 'I wouldn't have it any other way.'

'Ready for bypass.'

Max glanced back at the perfusionist seated at the table across from him, its myriad tubing and dials enough to make anyone nervous. But Gary Whitley—an expert in his field, Max had been told—was at the helm, his white goatee hidden beneath the surgical mask. 'Tell me when.'

Once they put Baby Hope on the bypass machine, the race with time would begin once again. The sooner the donor heart was in place and beating, the better chance the baby had for a good outcome. The risk for post-perfusion syndrome—the dreaded 'pump head'—grew the longer a patient was on bypass. Most of the time, the symptoms seemed to resolve after a period of weeks or months, but there were some new studies that suggested the attention and memory problems could be long-reaching for some individuals. Hopefully the baby's young age would preclude that from happening.

'Let's start her up.'

Gary adjusted the instrumentation and looked up just as the centrifugal pumps began whirling, sending the blood through the tubes and over into the oxygenator. 'On bypass.'

Max then nodded at Anna, who noted the time. She would keep an eye on the maximum time allowable and notify the team as they arrived at certain critical markers: one-quarter, the halfway mark and the three quarters mark, although he hoped they didn't cut it that close.

Using a series of clamps and scalpels, they finished unhooking Hope's defective heart, and, after checking and double checking the great vessels, they removed the organ from the opening in her chest wall.

'Ready for donor heart.' The new organ carefully changed hands until it reached Max. He checked it for damage, despite the fact that it had already gone through rigorous testing. He preferred to inspect everything himself...to know exactly what he was dealing with.

Was that one of the reasons he'd asked Annabelle to be involved in the surgery? Because he knew what to expect when they worked together?

Yes. But it was also because he knew this patient meant so much to her. Leaving her out after all the time, effort, and—knowing Annabelle—love she'd put into Baby Hope seemed a terrible act. Almost as if he were discarding her once she'd served her purpose.

That thought made him wince, but he quickly recovered.

Everything looked good. He measured the new heart for fit on the patient's left atrium and trimmed a tiny bit of tissue to ensure everything went together as it should. Then he set about the painstaking process of suturing it all back together.

'One half.' Annabelle's voice was calm and measured, giving no hint of what must be going through her mind. Things like, *Are we on track?* Or, *How long until I see those beautiful eyes of hers open?*

Max knew those fears all too well. He experienced them on each and every surgery. But for him to do his job, he had to put those thoughts aside and move systematically through the process. The worst thing he could do was waste precious time worrying about each and every possible outcome.

But Max couldn't help giving her a tiny piece of reassurance. 'We're a little ahead of schedule. As soon as I finish these final sutures we can begin warming her up.'

In his peripheral vision, he saw Annabelle's eyelids close as if she was relieved by the words. Then she squared up her shoulders and continued to watch both him and the clock.

When the last stitch was in place, Max looked at every vessel and each part of the heart, making sure he'd forgotten nothing. Only when he was completely satisfied did he give Gary the okay to start the warming process and begin weaning Hope off the bypass machine. Sometimes the weaning process itself would coax the new heart into beating, the return of blood flow triggering the electrical impulses, which would then start firing. The surgical suite was silent until Annabelle's voice again counted down the time. 'Three quarters.'

This time there was the tiniest quaver to her

tone. *Don't worry, sweetheart. Just give her a few minutes.*

Sweetheart?

He hadn't used that endearment when thinking about her in ages. And he shouldn't be thinking it now.

His gaze zeroed in on his patient's open chest to avoid glancing up at Annabelle, knowing something in his expression might reveal emotions he wasn't even aware of having.

Two more minutes went by. If the heart didn't start soon, they would have to shock it with the paddles. Even if it came to that, they could still have a good outcome, but something made him loath to use more aggressive measures.

Just one more minute. Come on. You can do it.

This time he couldn't resist glancing at Annabelle. Her face was tight and drawn, no colour to be seen, even in her lips. It was as if she were sending her own lifeblood over to the baby so that she could live.

His assessment of his wife's thoughts was

interrupted by a quick blipping sound from a nearby machine. Everyone's attention rocketed to the heart monitor. *Blip-blip.*

Looking directly at the new heart, he saw a beautiful sight. The organ contracted so strongly it seemed to want to leap out of its spot.

Within a few more seconds, it had settled into a normal sinus rhythm. Strong. Unfaltering. Unhesitating. The most beautiful sight he'd ever seen.

'It's working.'

There were cheers of relief throughout the operating theatre, but one voice was missing. When he looked up to see why, Annabelle's hand was covering her mouth and tears were streaming down her face. His instinct was to go to her, wrap her in his arms and say everything was going to be okay. But he couldn't promise her that. Not ever again. It was why they were no longer together, because he couldn't bring himself to say those words. He'd been at the end of himself by that point and had to let her go in order to save her.

At least that was Max's reasoning at the time. Had it been valid?

It didn't matter now. What was done was done. There was no going back. Not that he wanted to.

So he turned his attention to the patient in front of him, assessing her needs and checking the sutured vessels for any sign of leakage. Everything looked tight and steady. And that beautiful heart was still beating.

Five minutes later, the decision was made to close her up. Max could have passed that work over to someone else. In fact it was customary after a long surgery to let an intern do the final unglamorous job. But Max wanted to do it himself. Needed to follow the path all the way to the end before he would feel right about passing her over to the team of nurses who would watch over her all night long.

'Let's finish it.'

Soon the room was alive with different staff

members doing their appointed tasks, the atmosphere much different now than it had been twenty minutes ago when that heart had sat in Baby Hope's chest as lifeless as her old heart was now. They would start the immunosuppressant medication soon, to prevent her body from turning on her new organ and killing it, mistaking it for an invader. She'd be on medication for the rest of her life, which Max hoped would be a long and healthy one.

He set up the drainage tube system and then closed the sternum, using a plating technique that was made up of tiny screws and metal joiners. He carefully tightened each and every screw. Once that was done, muscle was pulled back into place and finally the skin, leaving space for the tubes that would drain off excess fluid. And the ventilator would remain in place for the next day or so, until they were sure everything was still working the way it should.

An hour later, an exhausted but jubilant Max cleared the baby to head to Recovery and then to the critical care ward to be closely observed over the next couple of days. Six hours of surgery had seemed like an eternity, at least emotionally. He was worn out.

When the baby was wheeled away, he congratulated his team, aware of the fact that Annabelle was standing in the corner. She looked as tired as he felt. A cord tightened in his gut as he continued thanking everyone individually.

The last person he went to shake hands with was the perfusionist, who had done his job perfectly, with stellar results. Only when he reached the man, his head was swivelled to the side, looking with interest at…

Annabelle.

He frowned.

Max peeled off his gloves and tossed them in the stack of operating rubbish that sat in a heap a few feet away, watching Annabelle. She was gathering instruments, seemingly unaware of the other man's gaze.

Gary's attention finally swung back to him

and he smiled, stretching his hand out. 'Were you waiting for me? Sorry. It was great working with you.' He nodded in Annabelle's direction. 'I was just wondering who the nurse was. She looks vaguely familiar, but I don't think I've seen her in surgery before.'

One of his biceps relaxed, and he accepted the man's quick handshake.

She wasn't using her married name any more, but he decided to use a tactful approach and see if the perfusionist understood his meaning. 'That's Annabelle Brookes-Ainsley. She works down in the neonatal unit, but was interested in this particular case.'

'Because...' The drawn-out word said Gary hadn't connected the last names yet.

'Because she's been working with this patient. And it's my first surgery here at the hospital. It was a chance to see me in action.' He connected the two phrases, even though one had nothing to do with the other. He certainly didn't want to spell out that Annabelle was his wife. He was pretty sure she wouldn't appreciate that, but the guy had put him in a tough spot.

'To see you in…' Gary's eyes widened and a hint of red crept up his neck. 'Of course. I should have realised.'

'Not a problem. I'll let you get back to what you were doing, but I wanted to come over and say how much I appreciate the smooth handling of this surgery.'

'I—well, I appreciate it.'

With a ghost of a smile, Max swung away from the man and spoke briefly with the intern who'd been observing, answering a couple of questions he had. He kept that easy smile, but his insides were churning to get to Annabelle before she disappeared. And she would, if he knew her. She would want to go see how Baby Hope was doing.

The heart transplant marked the third patient 'crisis' that she'd assisted him with, and in each instance she'd done her job with precision and without hesitation. Max found it amazing that two people who'd been through what they had could still pull together and work for the good of someone else.

No rancour. No snide remarks, just an uncanny ability to know what the other was thinking, probably ingrained from years of living together. Whatever it was, they'd worked well together.

Except it evidently didn't carry over to their 'off times' because Max had no idea what she was thinking now. He answered one final question and then glanced at where Annabelle had been a second ago. Except, just as he'd suspected, she wasn't there. She'd already left the room. Without a single word.

CHAPTER SIX

ANNABELLE WASN'T SURE where she was going, but she had to get away from that room. It wasn't just the pile of bloody gauze and surgical tools that bothered her. Or the sight of Hope's still form being wheeled out of the surgical suite. It was Max's easy handling of both the case and the surgical staff.

And the aftermath of an adrenaline high that would probably send her crashing back to earth over the next hour or so. She didn't want Max to see her like that. He'd seen it enough over the course of their marriage.

She got ten steps down the hallway when she heard her name being called. Annabelle stopped in her tracks.

Max. Of course it was.

He had always been too good at ferreting out her emotional state, picking up on the nuances of what she was feeling. Maybe if he hadn't been quite so adept at it, she would have been able to hide her anguish over her repeated miscarriages. Only she hadn't. So she'd resorted to pulling away emotionally in an attempt to hide it from him. And in doing so had driven a wedge between them that had been impossible to remove.

Steeling herself, she turned to face him.

He came even with her, looking down into her face. Searching for something. She had no idea what.

'Good job in there.'

That made her lips twitch. 'I didn't have a very difficult task.'

'No, but I know you had a vested interest in that baby. It couldn't have been easy watching the clock ticking without any idea of what to expect.'

'I've watched transplants being done before.'

He frowned. 'You have? Because Gary, our

perfusionist, doesn't seem to remember seeing you before.'

'I haven't actually watched one done at this hospital. Well…I mean, I've watched videos of them.' Lots of them actually. She'd wanted to see exactly what Hope would experience from start to finish.

'And did I measure up to what you saw in those videos?'

She sensed a slight hint of amusement in his voice. But yes, Max had measured up, damn him. Except she'd desperately wanted him to be as good as or better than anything that had passed across her computer screen. And he had been. His fingers had been nimble and yet gentle as he'd handled Hope, both before surgery and during it. There'd been a steely determination about him as those brown eyes had inspected the new heart. She'd seen it again as he'd waited for that same heart to begin beating. And then the smile he probably hadn't even realised he'd flashed when that tiny organ had started pumping oxy-gen-rich blood through Hope's tired body.

Watching him work had caused something warm to flood through her own insides. Just as the warmth had washed through Hope's veins as the surgery had neared completion. And that scared her.

'You already know the answer to that. Hope is alive because of you.'

That same devastating smile slid across his lips. 'It's been a while since I've done surgery in a hospital setting. Actually it's been a while since I've done anything in a modern hospital.'

Annabelle matched his smile. 'I'm sure it takes some getting used to after what you've seen.'

'It does.' He paused for a long moment and his eyes dipped to her mouth.

Annabelle's breath caught in her lungs. 'I can't imagine what it must have been like.'

Slowly his glance came back up to hers. 'You'd have to be there to really understand.' He paused for a moment. 'I actually have a Christmas fundraising gala to attend with Doctors Without Borders the day after tomorrow in London. If you're interested in learning more you could always come with me. Or are you slated to work two nights from now?'

'No, but…' Was he asking her to travel to London with him? Because it sure sounded like—

'I know we haven't made any hard and fast decisions about the future, but maybe we should. We could talk on the drive over.'

She stood there paralyzed, afraid to say no, but even more afraid to say yes.

'I would like you to come, Anna. Please.'

Oh, Lord. When he asked her like that, with his head tipped low to peer into her face, it was impossible to find the words to refuse him. So she didn't try. 'What about Hope?'

'We should be able to tell by tomorrow how things are going, and Sienna has already agreed to cover for me that night—along with her team, which she assures me is the best in the area.

We'll just be gone overnight. Hope will never even know we're gone.'

Overnight? That word sent a shiver through her, even though it shouldn't. Memories of other nights in London swirled to life in her head despite her best efforts. Of them in their flat, making love as if there were no tomorrow.

Of course, in the end, there hadn't been.

She shook herself back to reality. This was no big deal. And they did have a lot to discuss. Most fundraisers were held at night. By the time the festivities wound down and they got back on the road it would be late. Probably much later than Max would want to drive. And if there was alcohol involved…

They could stay at a hotel. Annabelle had done that on several occasions when she'd gone into London for a seminar or lecture in her field. It was no big deal. She'd travelled with colleagues before. They'd simply taken care of their own sleeping arrangements.

Would he bring the divorce papers with him

and sign them on the dotted line in front of her? If so, she should just let him. They both needed some closure, and maybe this would give it to them.

Even if the thought of taking that final step made her throat clog with emotion.

Why? It was time. Past time, actually.

'Okay, I'll go.' And she would just suck it up and muddle through the best she could. 'What kind of dress is it?'

'Black tie, actually.'

'Really? Isn't it too late to tell them you're bringing along a guest?'

'No.' He shrugged, the act making his shoulder slide against hers, a reminder of just how close he was standing. 'The invitation is for me and a guest. Most people bring a significant other.' That devastating smile cracked the left side of his mouth again. 'You're as close as I have to one of those.'

As in close, but no cigar? As in an almost-ex significant other?

'Ditto.' Her brows went up. 'I think.'

His hand came up, the backs of his knuckles trailing down the side of her face, leaving fire in their wake. 'We did good in that surgical suite. We gave her a chance that she wouldn't have otherwise had.'

'*You* did good. You made this happen.'

'Sienna could have done just as well.'

Annabelle was sure the other surgeon could have. But there had been something about the way Max had looked at that baby that had turned her inside out. Something more than simply a surgeon treating a patient. Hope had touched him as much as she'd touched Annabelle.

A wrench of pain went through her. Max would have made such a great father.

She'd wanted to do that for him more than anything. To give him what he hadn't been given by his own parents: the chance to watch a normal, happy childhood unfold. To love. And be loved. Only it hadn't worked out that way.

'Sienna didn't do it, though. You did.'

The fingers that had been slowly caressing her face curved around to the back of her neck.

Oh, Lord. He was going to kiss her. Right here in the hospital corridor. Was that the act of a man who was about to finalise a divorce?

Maybe. Weren't there exes who had sex as they travelled down the path to divorce?

Not her.

And yet, every nerve ending was quivering with awareness. With acceptance. Her lips parted.

'Sorry. Is your last name Ainsley?'

'Yes.' Their necks cranked around at the same time, foreheads colliding as they did so. Ouch. Damn it!

Only then did she remember that she didn't go by Ainsley any more.

She slid away from Max as a male nurse came towards them, horrified that she'd been caught red-handed flirting with her ex-husband.

He's not your ex. Not yet. And she wasn't flirting. She'd been… Oh, hell, she had no idea what either of them had been doing.

The nurse's eyes went from one of them to the other. Of course. He wasn't sure exactly who he was looking for. '*Max* Ainsley?'

'That would be you,' Annabelle said, glancing sideways at Max.

The nurse frowned. 'There's been a complication with the transplant patient.'

'Oh, God.' Annabelle's stomach clenched. She should have been in that room monitoring Baby Hope, not hanging around in the corridor mooning after her ex.

She hadn't been mooning. And she'd been heading for the recovery area when Max had stopped her to talk. Had asked her to go with him to some gala. Neither of them had expected the moment to morph into something more.

Didn't it always, though, where Max was concerned?

They hurried down the hallway following the retreating nurse. 'What do you think it is?'

'I have no idea.' He took his smartphone out of his pocket. 'No one tried to page me that I see.'

They arrived in Recovery, and Max slid through the door with Annabelle close behind. 'What's the problem?'

Two nurses were at the baby's head watching the heart monitor on the side. Annabelle saw it at once.

'A-fib.'

Her eyes swung to Max, waiting for his assessment. And the concern on his normally passive face sent a wave of panic through her.

Damn it!

Max went into immediate action. While post-operative atrial fibrillation was a fairly common complication of cardiac surgeries, POAF wasn't the norm for heart transplants, and, when it did show up, it typically showed up a couple of days down the line. That made it a very big deal. Especially in an infant that had already been in crisis in recent days.

The possibilities skated through his head and were legion. Problem with the pulmonary vein? Probably not. The isolation of that vessel usually helped prevent POAF. Acute rejection? Not likely this soon after transplantation. Pericardial inflammation or effusion? Yes. It could be that. Fluid could be building around the heart—the body's reaction to inflammation. And it could cause a-fib, especially if it came on this quickly.

'Let's see if she's got some effusion going on and work from there.'

The baby, awash in tubes and bandages, looked tiny as she lay in the special care incubator, a tuft of soft blonde hair turning her from a patient into a person. He glanced to the side to see that Annabelle's face was taut with fear, her hands clenched in front of her body.

Was she worried about losing this one, the way she'd lost baby after baby due to miscarriage?

He'd been helpless to prevent those, but he damned well wasn't right now. He could do something to turn this around. And if he had anything to do with it, this baby was going to live.

He belted out orders and over the next three hours they ran several tests, which confirmed his diagnosis. They pumped in anti-inflammatories, and he and Annabelle settled in to wait for a reaction. Four hours after the initial alarm was raised, Baby Hope's heart had resumed a normal sinus rhythm.

Annabelle sank into a rocking chair, her elbows propped on her knees, her back curving as she sat there with her eyes closed. 'Thank God.'

Unable to resist, Max went over and used his palm to move in slow circles between her shoulder blades. 'We'll keep a close eye on her over the next twenty-four hours, but I'm pretty sure we've got this licked. As long as the fluid doesn't start building again, the rhythm should hold.'

'And if it starts building?'

'We'll cross that bridge when we come to it, Anna.'

The other nurses had moved on to other patients, now that the crisis was over, leaving Max and Annabelle alone with the baby.

Annabelle reached into the incubator and smoothed down that tuft of hair he'd noticed earlier. The gesture caught him right in the gut, making it tighten until it was hard to breathe. 'I think you're too close to this case. Maybe you need to take a step back.'

'Social services handed me her care.' She glanced up at him. 'Please don't make me stay away.'

He could do just that. Let someone know that her emotions were getting in the way of her objectivity. And he probably should. But Max couldn't bring himself to even mention that possibility. He hadn't been able to comfort her during those awful times in their marriage, but he could give her this. As long as it didn't take too big a toll on her.

She was a grown woman. She could make her own decisions. Unless it adversely affected their patient.

'I won't. But I'm going to count on you to recognise when your emotions are getting the better of you and to pull back.'

He didn't say the words 'or else', but they hung
between them. Anna acknowledged them with a
nod of her head. 'Fine. But I don't think I should
go to the Christmas party with you.'

'Miss McDonald will take good care of her. If
she starts taking another turn tomorrow, we'll
both stay here. But it's only for one night. We'll
be back the next day.'

She looked up, her hand still on the baby's
head. 'Are you sure?'

Why he was so insistent on her going with him
he had no idea. But these first few days at the
hospital had been crazy. With the staff short-
ages, Annabelle had probably worked herself
almost into the ground. A little Christmas cheer
was in order. For both of them. They could count
it as a celebration of Hope's successful surgery.

He told her as much, and then added, 'I'll tell
you what. As long as she's holding her own,

we'll go to London. If we hear the slightest peep out of Sienna, we'll come back immediately. It's not that long a drive.'

Her thumb brushed back and forth over the baby's tiny forehead. 'Okay.'

She probably had no idea how protective she looked right now. As if her very presence were enough to keep anything bad from happening to that baby. If it worked like that, Annabelle might have three or four children by now.

His children.

Max's throat tightened, a band threatening to cut off his airway. There would be no children. Not for Annabelle. And not for him.

That had nothing to do with this case. Or with either of them. Max needed to remember that, or the past would come back and undo all the progress he'd made over the last three years.

Progress. Was that what it was called? His stints in Africa seemed more like running away.

No. He'd helped a lot of children during those trips. Kids that might have had no chance had he not been there.

Like Baby Hope?

It wasn't the same at all. Hope could have had any number of doctors perform her transplant. He'd just happened to be here at the time.

And he was glad he was.

His fingers gave Annabelle's shoulder a squeeze. 'She needs her rest.'

A ridiculous statement, since Hope was in a drug-induced sleep. He had a feeling his words were more to help Annabelle rest than the baby.

'She's just so…helpless.'

'She might be. But we're not. She's got a great team of experts who are pretty damned stubborn.'

'Like you.'

That made Max smile, the band around his throat easing. 'Do I fall on the expert side or the stubborn side?'

'Both.' She tilted her head back and smiled up at him. 'Hope is extremely lucky to have you on her team.'

'Thank you.'

When she stayed like that, he gave in to temptation and bent down to give her a friendly kiss, hoping to hell no one was looking through the observation window at them right now.

He straightened, his fingers moving beneath her hair to the warm skin of her neck, damp despite the chilly temperatures in the room. From the stress of working to keep Hope's a-fib from turning into something worse. She had to be absolutely exhausted. 'You need to get some rest too, Anna. Before you collapse.'

'I will.' Her attention moved back to the baby. 'I just want to sit here a little longer, okay?'

He had a feeling nothing he said was going to move her out of that chair, so he did something he shouldn't have done. Something that would only test his equilibrium more than it already had been.

He pulled up a second rocking chair and settled in beside her.

'How are the quads?'

Ella and Annabelle walked towards the front

doors of the local café just like they did every Friday morning. Only today big flakes of snow were beginning to fall around them, sifting over the Christmas decorations that had been strung to the lamp posts. It should have felt festive, like something out of a postcard. But it didn't.

She had too much on her mind for that.

She tightened the scarf around her neck, needing her friend's advice today. The midwife hadn't steered her wrong when she'd convinced her to move to the Cotswolds a year ago. The change in scenery had done her a world of good. At least until Max had come barrelling back into her life. But no one could have predicted that he would be the one taking Sienna's place. Well, Sienna had known, but, from her reaction when she realised they knew each other, the cardiothoracic surgeon had had no idea who he was when the hospital had contracted him.

Annabelle just had to think about how to broach the subject. So she'd started with something work related until she could figure out how to bring up Max's name.

'They're fine so far. Mum and babies all doing well. It's very exciting.'

Ella had seemed distracted over the last couple of weeks. But every time Annabelle tried to gently probe to see what was bothering her, her friend clammed up. 'I hope everything goes well for them.'

'Me too.' Ella pushed open the door to the café and got into line along with probably ten other people who were all ordering speciality coffees and breakfast sandwiches. 'So what's going on with Max?'

Whoa. So much for casually introducing the subject after an appropriate amount of small talk. But she should have known that wasn't going to happen. Ella tended to jump right to the heart of the matter. Except when it came to talking about her own issues, evidently. But at least she seemed to be feeling better than she had a couple of days ago. Maybe she wasn't catching the virus after all.

'What do you mean?'

'Are we really going to play this game, Annabelle?'

Her? Her friend had been pretty evasive herself recently.

'I guess we're not.' She gripped the wrought-iron rail that kept customers headed in the right direction. 'It's no big deal. He asked me to go to a Christmas fundraiser with him. It's in London.'

'He did? When did this happen?' Ella's face was alight with curiosity. And concern.

Annabelle couldn't blame her. Max had only been at the hospital a few days, but he'd already managed to turn her neat and orderly world on its head. Just as he always did. She'd sworn she was immune to him, that she could stay objective.

But just like with Baby Hope, it seemed that Max had the uncanny knack of being able to separate the fibres of her emotions and stretch them until Annabelle was positive they would snap.

He'd warned her about getting too emotionally attached to Hope. But who was going to warn her about him?

Max was a master at keeping his feelings under wraps. She knew the way she—and the rest of her family—wore her heart on her sleeve made him uncomfortable. His background had made him much more cautious about big emotional displays when they'd started dating. But with a lot of work and time spent with her parents that personality trait had turned around to the point that Max didn't think twice about slinging his arm around her shoulders. That was when Annabelle knew she could love him.

His parents had died when he was in his early twenties, before he and Annabelle met. Even his grieving had been a private affair. And when she'd lost her babies...

He'd gone back to being clinical. Probably because she'd been so overwrought the first time or two. Then she'd begun pulling away as well and it had snowballed from there. She'd called him heartless that last time.

No more, Anna.

Wasn't that what he'd said?

But had he really been as heartless as she'd thought? Maybe his grief—like with his parents' deaths—had been worn on the inside.

'Anna?'

Her friend's voice called her back. She tried to remember the question. When had Max asked her to the charity event? 'He asked me yesterday, after Hope's surgery.'

When he'd almost kissed her in the hospital corridor.

If the male nurse hadn't interrupted them when he had…

God! She was setting herself up for disaster.

The redhead moved forward several feet in line. 'How did he ask you?'

'Um…with his voice?'

Ella jabbed her with her elbow. 'That's not

what I mean and you know it. Was he asking you to a fundraiser? Or was he asking you to something else?'

Something else?

'I'm not sure what you mean.'

Ella turned her attention to the barista, ordering her usual beans and eggs breakfast with coffee.

Unlike her friend, Annabelle's stomach was churning too much to go for a hearty breakfast so she ordered a cup of tea and a couple of crumpets with butter and marmalade.

'What in the world are you having?' Her friend curled her nose, her Irish accent coming through full force, as it did when she was amused.

'I'm trying to eat lighter these days.'

Ella tossed her hair over her shoulder, taking the coffee the woman at the counter handed her. 'I'll go find us a table.'

It would do no good to try to hide anything from the midwife. She had always been far too good at seeing through her. Then again, there was that heart-on-the-sleeve syndrome that Annabelle just couldn't shake. The barista handed her a teapot and cup, promising that she would be along with their breakfast orders soon. There was nothing left but to join Ella and try to sort through all of her feelings about spending time alone with her husband tomorrow evening. After all the years they'd been apart, he shouldn't still leave her weak at the knees, but he did. And there was no denying it.

The second she sank into her chair, the midwife wrapped her hands around her chunky white mug and leaned forward. 'So tell me what's going on.'

'I'm not sure.'

Ella didn't respond, just sat there with brows raised.

Okay, so this was worse than just spilling her guts. 'Like I said, it's Max.'

This time her friend laughed. 'I thought we'd already established that. If the rumours about the newest—and sublimely hot—member of Teddy's tight-knit family are true, then he was spotted with his lips puckered, ready to swoop in on the always untouchable Annabelle. Some accounts of that story included a ringing slap to the face.'

Annabelle's eyes widened, shock moving through her system. 'People think I slapped him?'

'Not everyone. Some think you disappeared into the nearest supply cupboard with him.'

'Oh, heavens!' She poured tea into her cup and took a quick sip, letting the hot liquid splash into her empty stomach, hoping it would give her some kind of strength. 'Do they know who he is?'

She hoped Ella would understand the question. Did everyone at the hospital know that Max was her husband? Not that he actually was, except for on a piece of paper. The second she'd told him to get out, the marriage had been over.

'If they don't yet, they're going to work it out soon enough.' A waitress stopped by and dropped off their plates of food. 'The only thing stopping them is that you're using your maiden name. But of course, that makes it even more delicious as it heads down the gossip chain. Who wants to hear about an old married couple doing naughty things?'

'Great. So what do I do about it?'

'You might want to think about putting your own version of events out there so that you—and Max, for that matter—don't wind up with a real mess on your hands.'

'And what version of events is that? That I'm married to Max, but that we're on our way to dissolving the marriage? Talk about winding up with a mess on my hands.'

She already had. And she wasn't exactly sure what she could do to fix it. Especially since some people had evidently seen their display after the transplant surgery, when she was as sure as the next person that Max had been about to kiss her. If not for the nurse…

She presumed that he had been one of the ones to start the rumour. Then there was the situation of the actual kiss that had passed between them. But that had been outside the pub, and she was pretty sure no one from the hospital had been there. It was why she'd chosen the place.

Quickly telling Ella about that incident as well as all of the confusing feelings and emotions she'd been dealing with up to this point, she shrugged. 'Maybe I should have told him I wouldn't go to London with him.'

'Are you kissing...I mean kidding?' Ella grinned to show that the slip had been anything but an accident. 'You two have got to figure this thing out. There's obviously something there. That's what people are picking up on. Tell me you're not still in love with him.'

Annabelle didn't miss a beat, although her fingers tightened on the handle of her teacup. 'Of course not. But that doesn't mean I don't care what happens to him. I want him to be happy.'

'And you don't think he will be with you?' Ella took a deep breath. 'You've been locked in the past, Anna, whether you realise it or not.

I think you have a decision to make. If you really believe you shouldn't be together, and you want him to be happy, then maybe it's time to do something about it. Remove yourself as an obstacle, as hard as that might be.'

When she'd asked Max to leave, she'd made no effort to go after him. And he'd made no effort to come back and work things out. Besides, she'd been so devastated by the fact that he wasn't willing to sit and wallow in misery with her that she hadn't been thinking straight.

But he evidently hadn't needed to wallow. He could have fought for their marriage—offered to go with her to counselling. But he hadn't. He'd simply seemed relieved it was all over with.

Her heart clutched in her chest. She'd been relieved too. And now?

Now she didn't know how she felt.

Their food was long since gone, although Annabelle couldn't remember actually eating her crumpets. But she must have since the spoon from the little pot of marmalade was sitting on her bread plate, remnants of orange rind still clinging to its silver bowl.

'Maybe you're right. Maybe it is time to do something.' She could contact her solicitor and ask him to prod Max to sign, since she couldn't seem to get the nerve up to ask him herself.

'Unless you decide you still love him. Then I say you fight.' Ella reached across and squeezed her hand. 'I know that doesn't help, but maybe you need to take a closer look at your heart. See what it's telling you to do.'

'I don't think I can.' That kiss went through her mind. He was certainly still attracted to her, he'd said as much, but Annabelle had always assumed that he'd stopped loving her when he'd left their home. So even if she cared about him, would it matter?

'Maybe that gala will give you the strength to do just that. If it does, then you have a decision to make. And this time you'd better act on it, one way or the other. Unless you're content to remain in stasis for the rest of your life.'

No. Of that Annabelle was sure. She had been locked in a kind of suspended animation for three years now. It was time to move forward.

Even if that meant leaving Max behind. For ever.

CHAPTER SEVEN

MAX SAT ON the stairs, listening to his parents argue.

Again.

For the first time in his fifteen years he was scared about what might happen to him. Would they leave him here by himself?

'I am going on that cruise, whether you come with me or not.'

His dad's angry voice carried easily, just as it always did. Even if Max had been upstairs in his room, he would have heard those words.

'And what about Maxwell?'

'What about him? If you're worried, ask your aunt Vanessa to come and stay with him. I'm sure she'll be happy to lounge around the pool and do nothing.'

'Doug, that's not fair.'

'What's not fair about it? I consider it an equitable trade. I worked hard for this bonus, and I'm not going to give it up.'

There was a pause, and he held his breath as he waited for his mother's answer. 'Okay, I'll ask her. But we can't keep doing this. Vanessa has accused me more than once of not wanting him.'

'Just ask her.'

No reassurance that his parents actually did want him. They never took him on any of their so-called trips.

His hands tightened into fists as they rested on his knees. Then he slowly got up from his spot and crept back up the stairs. To pretend he didn't care.

Except when he got to his room and opened the door there was someone already in there. A woman...crouched on the floor beside his bed, crying. She looked up. Blue eyes met his.

Annabelle!

Suddenly he was grown up and his childhood bedroom morphed into the bathroom of their London flat. Anna held a small plastic stick in one hand, her eyes red and swollen. When he went to kneel down beside her to comfort her, she floated away. Through the door. Down the stairs, where everything was now eerily quiet. No matter how hard he tried to reach her, she kept sliding further and further away, until she was a tiny blip on the horizon. Then poof! *She was gone. Leaving him all alone. Just as his parents had.*

Max's eyes popped open and encountered darkness. He blinked a couple of times, a hand going to his chest, which was slick with sweat.

God. A dream.

He sat up and shoved the covers down, swinging his legs over the side of the bed.

Well, hell!

He didn't need a dream to tell him what he already knew.

But maybe his subconscious had needed to

send him a clear and pointed message about going to that Christmas party with Anna: that he needed to tread very, very carefully.

Baby Hope was still holding her own. And he'd finally shaken off the remnants of that dream he'd had that morning.

He'd also received some positive news about the accident victims they'd treated a couple of days ago. Several of the patients had already been released to go home, and the rest of them were expected to recover. Sarah, who'd been one of the most badly injured, might have to have surgery to stabilise the sternal fracture. But everyone was hopeful that she'd heal up without any lasting damage.

That was some very good news.

He hadn't seen Annabelle yet this morning. Which was another good thing.

Right, Max. Just because you've passed the entrance to the hospital multiple times since your arrival this morning, means nothing.

A thought hit him. Maybe she'd come down with the same virus that had plagued other hospital staff.

It didn't seem likely. A few of those had trickled back to work today, and no one else had called in sick. At least, that was what one of the nurses had told him. So it seemed that the outbreak might be dying down. A good thing too. The closer they got to Christmas, the more patients they'd probably be seeing. Everywhere he looked, there were doctors and nurses whose faces appeared haggard and tired.

Frayed nerves were evident everywhere, including the operating room this morning, where he'd had to repair a hole in a young patient's heart. The anaesthetist had snapped at a nurse who'd only been trying to do her job. He'd apologised immediately afterward, but the woman had thrown him an irritated glance, muttering under her breath. It was probably a good thing that he'd understood none of the words.

All of a sudden, Annabelle came hurrying

down the hall, a red coat still belted tightly around her waist. When she caught sight of him and then glanced guiltily at the clock to his right, one side of his mouth cranked up in spite of himself. She was late.

The Annabelle he knew was never late. Ever.

He moved a few steps towards her. 'Get held up, did you?'

'I'm only six minutes late.'

For Anna, that was an eternity. He held up his hands to ward off any other angry words. 'Hey, I was only asking a friendly question.'

'Sorry, Max. It's just been quite a day already.'

'Yes, it has.' His had started off with that damned nightmare, followed by a surgery at five o'clock this morning. Fortunately, the procedure had been pretty straightforward, and he'd been out of the surgical suite an hour later.

Her glance strayed to his face. 'What time did you get here?'

'A few hours ago.'

'I thought shift changes were at eight.' Her fingers went to her belt, quickly undoing the knot.

He nodded. 'They are. I had an emergency to see to, so I came in early.'

Her breath caught with an audible sound, her hands stopping all movement. 'Hope?'

'No, another surgery. It was urgent, but it came out fine.'

'I'm so glad.' She finished shifting out of her jacket and stepped into her office, where she hung the garment on the back of the door. Her lanyard was already hanging on a cord around her neck. 'Have you been to see Hope yet?'

'Once. She's still stable. I was just getting ready to check on her again. Care to join me?'

'Yes. I was halfway afraid something would go terribly wrong during the night.'

A cold hand gripped his heart. It had indeed. He shook off the thought.

'I would have called you, if something involving Hope had come up.'

She nodded. 'Thank you.'

'So your day has already been tough?'

'Kind of. I've been on the second floor.'

'Oncology?' Some kind of eerie premonition whispered through his veins.

'Yes.' Her voice quavered slightly. 'We found out this morning that one of my nephews has been diagnosed with a brain tumour. I went to ask Dr Terrill a few questions about the type and prognosis. Just so I could hear first-hand what he might be facing.'

He hadn't yet met any of the doctors or nurses on the second floor, as each area was kind of insulated from each other. 'I'm sorry, Anna. Who is it?'

'It's Nate. Jessica's son...the one I mentioned.'

A band tightened around his chest. 'How old is he?'

'Just two.'

Jessica, the youngest of Annabelle's sisters, had already had a couple of children by the time he'd left. In fact, the huge size of Anna's family was one of the things that had created such pressure on her to have children of her own. She would never admit it, but with each new niece or nephew the shadows in his wife's eyes had grown. She'd wanted so desperately what her sisters had...what her parents had had. If the family hadn't been so close, it might not have mattered quite so much. But they were—and it did.

He wanted to ask what Dr Terrill had said, but, at two years of age, the tumour had to be something that didn't take years to emerge.

'Jessica noticed he wasn't keeping up with his peers on the growth charts like he should. And recently he'd been complaining that his head hurt. So they ran a series of tests.'

Headaches could be benign or they could signal something deadly. 'Do they have the results?'

Annabelle could say it was none of his business. And it wasn't. Not any more. He'd lost the right to know anything about her family when he'd walked out of their home and flown to Africa.

'A craniopharyngioma tumour. They're in

discussing treatment options with their doctor today.'

He went through the catalogue in his head, searching for the name.

Found it.

Craniopharyngiomas were normally benign. But even though they didn't typically spread outside the original area, they could still be difficult to reach and treat.

'Why don't you get someone to cover you for a few hours, so you can be on hand if they need you? Or maybe you should go to London early.'

That might solve his dilemma about the Christmas party.

'I need to work. And Mum and Dad are there with Jessica and her husband. At this point there are too many people. Too many opinions.'

Kind of like with Annabelle's in-vitro procedures. There had always been someone in her family stepping up with an opinion on this or that. It hadn't bothered him at first, but as things had continued to go downhill Max had come to wish they would just mind their own business. A ridiculous mind-set, considering Max himself had hoped to have a family as large and connected as Annabelle's had been—and evidently still was.

'If you'd rather not go to the party—'

'I want to go. It'll give me a chance to run by and check in on Nate while I'm in London.'

'Of course.'

Well, if fate didn't want to help him, he was stuck. Besides, he didn't blame her for wanting to go, if it meant making a side trip to see them. It was doubtful her family would want him there, though. Not with everything that had happened. But he could think about that later.

He decided to change the subject. 'Are you ready to go see Hope?'

'Yes, just let me check in and make sure there are no other urgent cases I need to attend to.'

Five minutes later, they were in Hope's room, gowned and gloved to minimise exposure to pathogens that could put the tiny girl in danger.

She was still sedated, still intubated. But her colour was good, no more cyanosis. Something inside Max relaxed. Her atrial fibrillation hadn't returned after the scare yesterday, and her new heart was beating with gusto.

The empty chair next to the baby's incubator made a few muscles tense all over again. This child would never have a concerned loved one sitting beside her to give her extra love and care. At least not her mum.

As if Annabelle knew what he was thinking, she lowered herself into that seat, her gaze on the baby inside. She murmured something that he couldn't hear and then slid her hand through one of the openings of the special care cot. She stroked the baby's hair, cooing to her in a quiet voice. More muscles went on high alert.

Had she done this for each of her nieces and nephews? The fact that she would never hold a child she'd given birth to made him sad. And angry. Sometimes the world was just cruel, when you thought about it. Here was a woman who could give unlimited amounts of love to a child, and she couldn't have one.

But life wasn't fair. There were wars and starving children and terrible destructive forces of nature that laid waste to whole communities.

Annabelle glanced up at him. 'The difference between how she looked thirty-six hours ago and right now are like day and night.'

He remembered. He also remembered how they'd almost lost her an hour after her surgery.

But this tiny tyke was a fighter, just as Anna had said she was. She wanted to live. Her body had fought hard, almost as if she'd known that if she held on long enough, relief would come.

And it had.

Maybe life was sometimes fair after all.

He laid a hand on top of the incubator. 'And so far she's handling all of this like a champ.'

'Where will she go after this?'

The question wasn't aimed at him. But he felt a need to answer it anyway. 'I'm sure there are a lot of people who would take Hope in a second. She'll get a lot of love.'

'I hope so.'

'There's no chance that her mum will come back and want her later?'

'It's been over two weeks. She knew that Hope was born with a heart defect. There's always a chance, but if she'd wanted to find her, surely she would have come back to the hospital by now?'

He nodded. 'What do social services say?'

'That if her mum doesn't return, she'll be placed in a foster home and then put up for adoption.'

That brought up another point. He took his hand off the cot. 'You've never thought again about adopting?'

That had been another sticky subject towards the end of their marriage. She'd refused to even entertain the idea.

'My sister's experience made me afraid of going that route. But after spending so much time with Hope, I'm more open to it than I was in the past. Not every case ends in heartache, like Mallory's did. I don't know if I'd be able to adopt Hope, but surely they would let me consider another child with special needs. I love my nieces and nephews, but…' She stopped as if remembering that she had a very ill nephew.

She withdrew her hand, staring into the special care cot.

'But it's not the same. I get it.' He wanted to make sure she knew that there was nothing wrong with wanting someone of your own to love. He'd once felt that way about Anna. That she made his life complete in a way nothing else could, not even his work in Africa, as worthy as that might be. But in the end, his dream had been right about one thing: she hadn't wanted him to stay.

'You've probably seen plenty of needy children in Africa.'

'Yes. There are some incredible needs on that continent. I've sometimes wished…' He'd sometimes wished he could give a couple of kids a stable home without poverty or fear, but with the way his parents had been… Well, it wasn't something he saw himself tackling on his own.

Then there was the unfinished business with Annabelle. It didn't lend itself to making a new start. Especially when the previous chapter was still buzzing in the background. It was another thing his dream had got right. Annabelle was out of reach. She had been for a long time. He needed to sign those papers. Only then could he move forward.

He'd been thinking more and more along those lines over the last several days. She was here. His excuse of old was that he wasn't quite sure where to find her. But that no longer held water.

He couldn't have hired a solicitor to track her down back then? Or have gone through her parents?

Probably. But he'd believed if she wanted that divorce badly enough, she would find him.

'You've sometimes wished what?'

'That I could make life better for a child or two.'

She swivelled in her chair, her face turning up to study his. 'You once told me you no longer wanted children.'

Yes, he had. After her last miscarriage, he'd told her that to protect her health and to save what was evidently unsalvageable: their marriage. So he'd told a lie. Except when he'd said the words, they hadn't been a lie. He'd just wanted it all to stop.

And it had.

'I was tired of all the hoops we had to leap through. Of all of the disappointment.'

'I'm so sorry, Max.' Her face went from looking up at him as if trying to understand to bending down to stare at the floor.

What the hell?

Realising she might have misunderstood his words, he knelt down beside her in a hurry, taking her chin and forcing her to look at him. 'I wasn't disappointed *in* you, Anna. I was disappointed *for* you. For both of us. I wanted to be able to snap my fingers and make everything right, and when I couldn't… It just wore me down, made me feel helpless in a way I'd never felt before.'

'Like Jessica must feel right now with Nate.' Her eyes swam with moisture, although none of it spilled over the lower rim of her eyelids.

'She has a great support network in you and the rest of the family.' Something Max hadn't felt as if he'd given to Annabelle. He'd withdrawn more and more of his emotional support, afraid to get attached to a foetus that would never see the light of day. And towards the end, that was what he'd started thinking of them as. Foetuses and not babies. And he'd damned himself each time he'd used that term.

'She does. Her husband has been her rock as well.'

Unlike him? His jaw tightened, teeth clenching together in an effort to keep from apologising for something that he couldn't change.

Her eyes focused on him. And then her hand went to his cheek. 'Don't. I wasn't accusing you of not being there, Max. I was the one who pulled away. You did what you could.'

'It wasn't enough.'

Her lashes fluttered as her lids closed and her hand fell back to her side. 'Nothing would have been enough. I was a mess back then. I'm stronger now.'

She was. He saw it in the way she cared for Baby Hope and the rest of her patients. She'd called Jessica's husband a rock. She could have been describing herself.

'You were always strong. They were just difficult days.'

Baby Hope stirred in her cot, one of her arms jerking to the side until her fingers were pressed against the clear acrylic of the incubator. Annabelle touched her index finger to the barrier separating her from the baby. 'This is the strong one. I'm envisioning a bright future for her.'

'She has a great chance.'

Annabelle sucked down a deep breath and let it out in a rush. 'Thank you for all you did to help her.'

'She did most of the work. She stuck around until we could find a donor heart.'

'Yes, she did.'

Max stood up and held out his hand, the ominous warning of his dream fading slightly. 'Let's let her get some rest.'

'Good idea. I need to get to work and then check in with my sister.' She took his hand, their gloves preventing them from feeling each other's skin, but it was still intimate, her grip returning his. He found himself continuing to hold her hand for several seconds longer than necessary. 'You'll let me know if there's any change in her condition, won't you?'

'You know I will.' He paused, not sure how she would feel about what he was about to say. 'You'll let me know about Nate, won't you? I know I've never met him, but I care about your family.'

He had loved her parents and siblings, had liked seeing what it was like to be part of a large and caring family. It had had its downsides as well, the births of her nieces and nephews seeming to increase Annabelle's anguish over her own lack of having babies, but that hadn't been anyone's fault. As upset as he'd been at times over what he'd seen as meddling, he was grateful her family had been there to give her the support he'd never had as a child and couldn't seem to manage as an adult.

'I will. And thank you.'

With that, Annabelle peeled off her gloves, threw them in the rubbish bin, and went out of the door.

'You go to the party, honey.'

Annabelle clenched her phone just a little tighter. 'Are you sure, Mum? I can spend the night there with you instead.'

'Don't do that. Nate is fine. He's resting comfortably right now.'

'And Jessie and Walter?' Her sister had to be frantic with worry. With a husband who travelled five days a week, it couldn't be easy to deal with a child's health crisis while his father worked to make a decent living.

'Walter is staying home this week. They're setting up timetables with their team of doctors. It looks like Nate's prognosis is better than it could have been. The tumour is not malignant, and they're hopeful they can get all of it with surgery.'

Even though it wasn't malignant, meaning it wouldn't spread wildly through Nate's body, it could still regrow, if they didn't get absolutely every piece of it when they operated. But resecting a tumour and differentiating between tumour cells and healthy tissue was one of the hardest jobs a surgeon had. At least with Baby Hope's surgery, once the transplant was done, there was no growth of foreign tissue to contend with. There were other problems that could arise, yes, like her a-fib, but cells of the old heart wouldn't hang around and cause trouble later. Once it was out of the body, it was gone for good.

She hadn't told her mum yet that Max was working at her hospital or that he was the one she was going to the party with. Somehow she needed to break the news to her. But she wasn't sure if she should do it now, with the worry of Nate hanging over her head. The last thing her mother needed was to lose sleep over another of her children. Her family had been shocked—and horrified—when they'd heard that she and Max had separated. So she had no idea how her mum would react. She'd probably be thrilled... and hopeful. Something else Annabelle didn't want her family being. She and Max were not getting back together.

'Who are you going with? Ella?'

Oh, great. Here it came.

'No. Not Ella.' She'd better just get it over with. 'I'm actually going with Max.'

There was a pause. A long one. Annabelle

could practically hear the air between their two phones vibrating.

'Mum? Are you there?'

'I'm here.' Another hesitation. 'I didn't know he was back in England.'

'He came back a week ago.' She bit her lip. This was turning out to be harder than she'd expected.

'Okay, then. I didn't know you'd been in contact with him.'

Oh, yes. Much harder.

'By coincidence, he's come to work at the same hospital as I am, here in Cheltenham.' Before her mother could jump to conclusions, she hurried to finish. 'He wound up here quite by accident. He's taking another surgeon's place while she goes on maternity leave.'

'You're positive he didn't know you were there?'

And there was that note of hopefulness she'd been hoping to avoid.

'Yes, I'm absolutely positive.'

'I wonder…' Her mother let whatever she was going to say trail off into nothing. Then she came back. 'Why don't you and Max come to London a little earlier? We're just getting ready to put up the tree and decorate it. You didn't help us put on the ornaments last year, and you know everyone would love to have you there. And Max, of course. Nate… Well, he would love it.'

Oh, Lord, how was she going to get out of this? She'd had no idea her mother would suggest she come over and help decorate the tree. Especially not with her ex in tow.

'I'm not sure Max will want to—'

'It certainly can't hurt to ask. And if he doesn't want to join us, he can just pick you up at the house later and off you'll go to the party.' Another pause, quicker this time. 'What kind of party did you say it was?'

'A Doctors Without Borders fundraiser.'

'Isn't that who Max left—I mean worked with?'

Her mum was right. Annabelle might have

been the one to ask him to leave, but Doctors Without Borders had been Max's escape route. They had used to talk about going and working together. But in the end, Max had gone alone.

'Yes.'

'Is he going back with them once he's finished his contract at the hospital?'

Something in Annabelle's stomach twisted until it hurt. No, that had been her, clenching her abs until they shook. She'd asked him that same question at the pub. 'I don't know what his plans are after that, Mum.'

'So this might be our last chance to see him for a while?' Her mum called something to her father, but she couldn't hear what it was. Great. She could only hope that she wasn't telling him that Max was back and that it would be good to have the family together again.

Her mum knew that Max had left, but she'd never told her that she'd served him with divorce papers soon afterwards. It had been a painful time in her life and she'd kept most of it to herself. And then as time had gone on and Max hadn't sent his portion of the paperwork back, it was as if Annabelle had put it to the back of her mind like a bad dream that had happened once and was then forgotten.

This probably wasn't a good time to bring up the fact that a reconciliation was highly unlikely. Max had given no indication that he wanted to get back together with her. In fact, even when he'd towed her from the restaurant and kissed her in the park, he'd referred to what was going on between them as 'the spark'. Physical attraction. People could be attracted to each other without it going any deeper than that.

'I'll ask him. But don't be disappointed if he'd rather not come, Mum.'

'I won't. But you'll come, even if he chooses not to, won't you?'

There was no way she was going to be able to get out of it. And actually she didn't want to. This was a family tradition that she'd participated in every year except for the last one, when she'd just been getting situated at Teddy's and had been too busy with all the changes to be able to take a train home to London. With Nate's diagnosis, though, she had to go. 'I'll be there, Mum, but I probably won't be able to stay for dinner.'

'Of course not. Tell Max I'm looking forward to seeing him.'

Okay. Hadn't she just explained that he might not want to come?

She would invite him. And then let him decide what he wanted to do. And if he agreed to go? Well, she'd have to decide how to tell him that her family wasn't privy to one small detail of their relationship: that not only had she asked him to leave, but she'd also asked him for a divorce. And the only thing lacking to make that happen…was Max's signature on a piece of paper.

'You what?'

Sitting in front of Annabelle's mum and dad's

house, Max wasn't sure what on earth had possessed him to say yes to this crazy side trip. Because he was suddenly having second thoughts.

Especially now.

'You didn't tell them we're divorcing?' The words tasted bitter as he said them, but how could she have neglected to tell her parents that their marriage was over, and that it had been her choice?

Surely they'd realised, when he'd never come home…

'There just never seemed to be a good time to mention it. Someone was always being born. And then my aunt Meredith passed away a year and a half ago. My dad retired six months after that. It's just been—'

'Life as usual in the Brookes' household.' He remembered well how frenetic and chaotic things got, with lots of laughter and some tears. It had taken him a while to get used to the noise—and there was a lot of it—but the love they had for each other had won him over. Especially when they had drawn him into the fold as if he'd always been a part of their close-knit group. It was what he'd always wanted, but never had. He'd been in heaven. While it lasted.

'Please don't be angry. I'll tell them eventually. Probably not tonight, since it's Christmas time, and with Nate's illness…'

'It's okay. Maybe it's easier this way. They did know we weren't living together any more.'

'They knew we'd separated, yes, of course. I left our flat and came home before moving to the Cotswolds.'

'Yes, the flat…' He almost laughed. Well, he guessed they were even, then, because there was something he hadn't told her either. That he hadn't sold the flat once she'd moved out of it, even though his monthly cleaning lady had called him to let him know Annabelle was moving home and that she'd said he could do what he wished to with the flat. Those words had hit him right in the gut. Somehow he'd never been able to picture her moving out of the place they'd turned into a home. He'd assumed he would sign the place over to her once the paperwork was finalised. But then she'd moved out. And the paperwork had never been signed.

Why was that?

'What about it?' Annabelle turned to him, her discomfiture turning to curiosity.

'We still have it, actually.'

Her head cocked. 'Still have it?'

'I never got around to selling it.'

Her indrawn breath was sharp inside the space of his small sports car. 'But why?'

That was a question he wasn't going to examine too closely right now. 'I was overseas on and off and it got pushed to a back burner. As time went on, well, it just never happened.'

'Who's living there?'

'No one. I never sublet it. Suzanne cleans it once a month, just like always. When repairs are needed, her husband comes over and does them.' He shrugged. 'I halfway thought maybe I'd return to London at some point.'

Except every time he'd got close to thinking about his home city, he somehow hadn't been able to bring himself to come back and visit. Instead, he'd landed in several different cities in between his stints with Doctors Without Borders.

Annabelle smiled and it lit up the inside of the car. 'I'm glad. I loved that place.'

'So did I.' Well, they were going to look awfully out of place at a tree-decorating party with their fancy clothes on. But she'd seemed so uncomfortable when she'd relayed her mother's request that he hadn't wanted to make her feel even worse—or have to go back to her mum and tell her that he'd refused to take part. That would have been churlish of him. At least now he knew why the invitation had been extended. If they'd been divorced, Max was pretty sure he'd have been persona non grata in this particular family, even if he hadn't been the one to initiate it.

Climbing out of the car, he went around to Annabelle's side and opened it for her. Out she stepped, a vision in red. Until she tried to move to the side so he could close the door and tripped over the hem of her gown, careening sideways. He grabbed her around the waist, his fingers sliding across the bare skin of her back as he did so.

Her momentum kept her moving and her arms went around his neck in an effort to regain her footing. 'Oh! Max, I'm so sorry...'

Just then the front door to the house opened, and people poured out of the opening, catching them tangled together.

Not good.

Because it didn't look as if he'd just been saving her from a fall. It looked as if they were having a private moment.

Not hardly.

Annabelle saw them at the same time as he did and quickly pulled back. So fast that she almost flung herself off balance all over again. He kept hold of her for a second or two longer to make sure she had her footing. Then they were surrounded by her family, and Annabelle was hugging various adults and squatting down to squeeze little ones of all sizes. He couldn't prevent a smile. This was the Annabelle he remembered, uncaring of whether or not her dress got dusty. The people she loved always came first.

Just as he once had.

He'd forgotten that in all of the unhappy moments that had passed between them. These had been good times. Happy times. And…he missed them.

George Brookes came around and extended his hand. 'Good to see you, Maxwell.' His booming voice and formal use of his name was just like old times as well. There wasn't a hint of recrimination on the man's face. Or in his attitude. Just a father welcoming his son-in-law for a typical visit.

Max squeezed his hand, reaching over to give him a man's quick embrace, then gave himself over to greeting the family he'd once been a part of.

Bittersweet. He shouldn't have come. And yet he was very glad he had.

Jessica came up to hug him. He held her shoulders and looked into her face. 'How are you and Walter holding up?'

Her chin wobbled precariously, but she didn't start crying. 'We're doing better now that you and Annie are home.'

Home.

Yes, he'd once considered this the home his childhood abode never was. And the Brookeses had been the family he no longer had. Despite his own parents' faults, he suddenly missed them. Regretted never once visiting their graves.

Once he'd lost the right to be a part of Annabelle's family, the children of Africa had become his family. And they had loved more freely and with more joy than anything he'd ever seen. They'd taught him a lot about unconditional love.

Something he'd never really given to anyone. Even Anna. He'd always held something back, afraid of being hurt. And in the end, he'd demanded she give up something she dearly wanted.

He'd been wrong in that. Even though he'd told himself time and time again that it had been to save Annabelle the pain of future miscarriages, maybe he'd been more interested in saving himself.

He didn't have time to think about it for long, though, because he was soon whisked back into the bosom of a family he'd dearly missed, sitting on the arm of the sofa while Annabelle and her sisters held up ornament after ornament, reminiscing about where each had come from. Some were home-made. Some were fancy and expensive. But each held some kind of special meaning to this family.

Anna was gorgeous in her flowing red gown. Off the shoulder, but with some loose straps that draped over her upper arms, it fitted her perfectly, the snug top giving way to a full loose skirt that swished with every twitch of her hips.

And they twitched a lot. Every once in a while she threw him a smile that was more carefree than any he'd seen from her in a long, long time. He knew that smile. She'd once worn it almost constantly. When he'd come home from work. When they'd gazed at each other across the dinner table. When they'd made love deep into the night…

His throat tightened, and he dipped a finger beneath his bow tie in an effort to give himself a little more room to breathe, even though he knew that wasn't the problem. In his hands, Max held the long white gloves Anna planned on wearing to the party, but had taken off so she wouldn't drop and break any ornaments. In the back of all their minds was Nate and his diagnosis, but when Max looked at the little blond boy, he was smiling and laughing on the floor as he played with his siblings and cousins. Suddenly Max wished he could commit this scene to memory so that he would never forget this moment.

When Nate got up from his place on the floor and came to stand in front of him, looking at him with curious eyes, the tightness in his throat increased.

'Where's my ball?'

He blinked. Max wasn't sure why the boy was asking him, but he was not about to refuse him. 'I don't know.'

'You help find?'

'Sure.' Getting to his feet, he tucked Anna's gloves into his pocket and held out a hand to the little boy. As he did, his doctor's mind took in the subtle signs of illness. Nate's small stature, the frailness of his fingers beneath Max's. Jessica sent him a look with raised brows.

'He's looking for his ball?' Max had to raise his voice to be heard.

'It's in the basket by the far wall in the dining room.' Jessica glanced at her son, the raw emotion in her eyes unmistakable. 'Thanks, Max.'

'Not a problem.'

Together he and the boy made their way into

the dining room. It looked the same as it always had, polished cherry table laid with glistening china and silver for the meal they would be having later. Gloria had never been worried about breakage, even with such a large and active family. His own mum had rarely set out the good china.

'There's the basket, Nate. Let's see if Mum was right.'

A white wicker chest was pushed against a wall, a large contingent of photographs flowing up and around it until they filled the space with black and white images.

Above the pictures ornate black letters gave a message to all who dined there.

In Stormy Seas,
Family Is A Sheltered Cove.

And it was. This family represented safety. Too many faces to count, but there must have been thirty frames, each telling a story. The birth of a child. The winning of trophies. The weddings of each of the girls. Jessica and Walter, Paula and Mark, Mallory and Stewart...

No. His heart caught on a stuttered beat, and he couldn't stop himself from moving closer. Annabelle and Max.

That day was pinned in his memory, superseding even his most recent ones. Anna, fresh from his kiss, was staring up at him with eyes filled with love. And he was... He had his arm wrapped around her waist as if he was afraid she might wander away from him if he didn't keep her close.

And she had. They'd both wandered.

Annabelle said she hadn't told her parents about the divorce. He wasn't sure if Gloria just hadn't had a picture to replace this one with, or if she'd left it up in hopes that one day he and her daughter might mend their fences and get back together.

Little did she know that those fences had been irrevocably broken. His gaze moved over the rest of the pictures. There were no others of them.

Maybe because they hadn't had all that much to celebrate during their marriage.

Part of that was his fault. They'd been fixated on having a baby for so long, they'd never made time to look at the other things they'd shared.

A small hand tugged on his. 'My ball? In basket.'

That was right. He'd forgotten about Nate and his ball. Forcing the lump in his throat to shift to the side, he gave the child a smile. 'Let's see if it's where Mum said it was.'

He opened the basket to find children's toys of every shape and size. Gloria must keep them for all of the grandkids to play with while they visited. And all of Annabelle's sisters now had children. Except for her.

He glanced through the doorway to see her still helping to decorate the tree, laughing at something someone had said. She was truly beautiful. Inside and out.

She seemed to have made her peace with not having kids. At least from what he could tell. So maybe it was time for him to accept that as well and start finding the joy in life. Turning back to his task, he found Nate trying to lean over the basket to get a green spongy ball the size of a football. 'Is that it, buddy?'

Grabbing the object from the chest, he handed it to Nate, who let go of his hand and gripped the item to his chest. 'Ball!'

'I guess we got the right one. Watch your fingers.' He carefully lowered the lid and latched it to keep small hands from getting pinched. They made their way back to the room and Nate went straight to Jessica, showing her his prize.

'Wonderful. You've found it!' She glanced up at Max with a mouthed, 'Thank you.'

He gave her a nod in return. Annabelle handed an ornament to her dad, who still stood ramrod straight and tall, probably from his days in the military. He gave her a quick hug and took the item, stretching up to put it on the very top of the tree. The man then turned towards the rest of the people assembled. 'Shall we light it before Annie and Max have to leave?'

A roared 'Yes!' went up from all the kids, making the adults smile. He glanced at his watch. Seven-thirty. The gala started in half an hour, so they did need to leave soon, since the party was on the other side of the city.

Annabelle came over to stand beside him.

With the flick of a switch all the lights in the living room went off, leaving them in darkness. An affected *'oooooh'* went up from the people gathered there.

Max stood there, the urge to put his arm around Anna's waist almost irresistible. The way he'd done in years past. He fought it for a moment or two, then gave up. His contract wasn't for ever. Once Sienna came back from maternity leave, he would be on his way again. So why not do this while he still could?

He slid his hand across the small of her back, the warm bare skin just above the edge of the fabric brushing against his thumb. Curving his fingers around the side of her waist, he was surprised when she reciprocated, her arm gliding around his back, leaning into him slightly as she smiled at something else her father was saying.

Then, just as suddenly as the overhead lights had been turned off, another set of lights flicked on. Swathed in layers of tiny glowing bulbs, the Christmas tree lit up the whole room like magic.

Not 'like' magic. It *was* magic. The tree. The night. The family. It was as if he'd never left three years ago. He didn't know whether to be glad or horrified. Had he not moved forward even a little?

No, he'd done nothing to forge a life without Anna. But he needed to either do just that, or…

Or try to do something to make things right between them.

Only, Max wasn't sure that was a good idea. They'd wounded each other without even trying. Wouldn't they just take up where they'd left off and do it all over again, if given half a chance? Wouldn't she ask him to leave once again?

He didn't know. All he knew was that he wanted to live here in this moment. Surrounded by Annabelle's family and the life and love they shared between them.

Except they needed to leave, if they were going to make it to the gala in time.

As if reading his thoughts, Annabelle looked up at him, her eyes shining with a strange glow that was probably due to the lights on the tree. 'We should go.'

'Are you sure you don't want to stay here and eat with your family?'

She lifted a handful of the fabric of her dress. 'We got all dressed up, so let's just enjoy the night. Okay? No expectations. No preconceived ideas.'

That shocked him. Annabelle was by nature a rigid planner. The attempts to get pregnant had been accomplished with clinical precision—the spontaneity wiped out more and more with each new wave of treatment.

If she hadn't just said those last words, he

would have assumed she was following through with what they'd planned to do. But something about the way she said it…

Well, if that was what she wanted, who was Max to disagree? And maybe it was the twinkle lights messing with some rational part of his brain, or the fact that her dress clung in all the right places, but he suddenly wanted to have Annabelle all to himself.

CHAPTER EIGHT

THE GALA HAD some twinkle lights of its own. Everywhere she looked there were signs of Christmas. From the garland-draped refreshment tables to the large ornate tree in the corner, filled with presents. Those boxes, mostly filled with toys and hygiene supplies, would make their way to needy kids all over the globe. Max had brought a small gift too, placing it gently under the tree.

'What is it?'

'A couple of toy cars.' He smiled at her. 'Not very practical.'

She smiled back at him, touched by his thoughtfulness. 'Some little boy is going to love it. Especially since it's *not* practical.'

When Max had suggested staying at her parents' house, she'd heard what she thought was a note of yearning in his voice. She'd been so tempted to just fall back into old patterns, but her parents might have started asking some harder questions if they'd stayed for the meal. Questions she didn't have the answers to. Or maybe she simply hadn't wanted to face those answers.

So here she was, with her ex-husband, at a party. And she had no idea what she was going to do about him.

No expectations. Wasn't that what she'd said?

Yes. So she was simply going to enjoy this night. Max was right. She'd worked herself into the ground over the last couple of weeks. Didn't she deserve to just let her hair down and have a little fun? He'd suggested using this time to celebrate Hope's successful surgery, so she would. And maybe she'd even send a wish up to the universe that the baby have a long and happy life.

That was what she'd do. She'd worry about what happened tomorrow when it came.

But for now, they had the whole evening in front of them, and she intended to enjoy it.

'Do you want something to drink?' Max's voice brought her back from wherever she'd gone.

'I'd love a glass of red wine, if they have it.'

'Wait right here. I'll go and see.'

He went off in the direction of the bar where there was quite a large crowd waiting to get something. He'd be up there for a while. She took the opportunity to study her surroundings.

Were all of these people doctors who volunteered with the organisation? Surely not. Some of them must just be donors who were here to pledge their support. Or people like her who simply wanted to know more about what happened in the places those volunteers served.

A leader board hovered over the raised platform to the left. Annabelle assumed they would unveil an amount at the end of the evening. There were also wooden boxes at all of the doors where you could drop in either a pledge card or a one-time donation. She'd gone to do just that when they'd arrived at the building, but Max had stopped her. 'I didn't bring you here for that.'

'I know you didn't.'

She'd wanted to give. Annabelle had often thought of going on one of the medical missions with the organisation, but, once she and Max had separated, the idea had been put on a back burner. Maybe she should rethink that. She glanced at the bar again. He was still waiting so maybe she could find some more information in the meantime.

She took the opportunity to move over to one of the doors where the boxes were, along with some colourful brochures about the organisation. Taking her purse out of her clutch bag, she pulled out several notes and dropped them into the slot of the box in front of her, then she went to peruse the pamphlets.

'What can I help you with?' A voice to her right made her look up.

A man in a tuxedo stood there, hand outstretched. 'I'm Dale Gerrard.' He flashed a set of very white teeth. 'I should warn you that I'm a recruiting agent for Doctors Without Borders. And I'm very good at my job. Are you in the medical profession?'

'I'm a nurse.' She accepted his handshake, although it felt weird doing so with her long white gloves in place.

The man epitomised the meaning of 'tall, dark and handsome.' With raven-black hair and tanned skin, he probably had more than his share of female admirers. He smiled again, giving her hand a slight squeeze before releasing it. 'Have you been on a mission with us before?'

'No. But I've thought about it in the past.'

'Really?' His level of interest went up a couple of notches. 'What stopped you?'

And that was something she wasn't about to tell him. It was too personal. And too painful. She glanced back at the line. Max was still over there. But just as she caught sight of him he suddenly turned, his eyes sweeping the crowd. Probably wondering where she'd gone.

And then he saw her. Just as the man next to her touched her arm to get her attention. Even from this distance she saw Max's brows pull together.

She looked away in a hurry, trying to focus on what the person beside her was saying. He was trying to hand her a clipboard and a pen.

Taking it with fingers that suddenly shook, she tried to corral her emotions. So what if Max had seen her? Surely he didn't think she'd stood around pining for him year after year.

What had started off as an enjoyable evening morphed into something different as a wave of irritation slithered through her innards. They weren't together any more, so Max had no say in her life. None.

Lifting her chin, she focused again on the man next to her. 'Yes, I would love to fill one out.'

'Great. Why don't you come behind the table with me and you can have a seat while you do?'

So Annabelle did just that, following Dale around the edge of the table where there was a line of seats, although no other representatives were there at the moment.

She sat down, suddenly glad to let her shaking legs have a break. Then she ducked her head and did her best to concentrate on the questions on the form, filling them in and hoping that Max didn't storm over here and embarrass her.

He wouldn't.

Her ex had never been a particularly jealous type. And there was no reason for him to start now. Especially since they were no longer a couple.

She was scribbling something in the box of the sixth question when a glass of red wine appeared in front of her. Swallowing hard, she glanced up. How had he got back that fast?

Sure enough, Max was standing in front of the table, taking a sip of whatever amber liquid was in his glass. 'Are you thinking of going on a medical mission?'

'I… Well, I…'

Dale, probably realising something was amiss, smoothly filled in the blanks. 'Annabelle was filling out a form to get more information on what we do.' He glided to his feet and offered his hand. 'I don't know if you remember me. I'm Dale—'

'I remember you. You were in Sudan with me two years back.'

'That's right. I haven't been back in a while. I'm doing recruiting work now.'

Max was gracious enough to smile at the man. 'And you're doing a great job of it, from what I can see.'

Looking from one to the other of them, Dale thanked him, and then said, 'I take it you two know each other.'

'You could say that.' His smile grew. 'Annabelle and I are married.'

'You're…' All the colour leached out of the man's face, leaving it a sickly grey colour. 'I didn't realise…' He glanced down at the form she was filling out. She had indeed put Annabelle Ainsley. She'd thought about using her maiden name, like at the hospital, but Ainsley had just seemed to flow out of the pen of its own accord. She had no idea why, but right now she could clobber Max for making this poor man feel like an idiot. Except a tiny part of her wondered why he'd spoken up and claimed she was his wife. He could have just played it off with a laugh and said that, yes, they knew each other from long ago. It would have been the truth, and it might have saved everyone some embarrassment. And yet he hadn't. He'd spoken the truth, without actually speaking it. Because they had not been husband and wife for almost three years.

Dale recovered, though. 'Well, maybe you can go on the next mission together, then. And since you already know the ropes, I'll let you help Annabelle finish filling out the form. I'm sure you can answer any questions as well as I can.'

With that, the man headed over to another person who was glancing at the literature, engaging him in conversation.

'Why did you do that?' She peered up at him.

'He's a flirt. I was trying to save you from being hit on.'

'Maybe I wanted to be hit on.' That was unfair. She didn't want to be. But she also didn't want Max taking it upon himself to be her rescuer when he hadn't been in her life for almost three years.

His gaze hardened. 'Did you?'

And it now came down to telling the truth. Or lying just to get back at him. 'No. But I could have handled it on my own.'

'I'm sorry, then.'

Annabelle let her emotions cool down. No harm done. And maybe he really had been trying to keep her from landing in an awkward situation. 'It's okay. And thank you for the wine.' She picked up the glass and took a sip.

'Did you really want to fill out a form?'

'I did. I've thought about volunteering in the past, but it never worked out.'

Max came around the table and dropped into the chair that Dale had vacated. 'I remembered us talking about it years ago. I thought you only said that because it was something I wanted to do.'

'It's been in the back of my mind for a while. I just never got around to doing anything about it.'

The sleeve of his tuxedo brushed against her upper arm as he leaned over to see what she'd filled out so far, his warm masculine scent clinging to her senses in a way that no one else's ever had. If Max had been worried about Dale, he needn't have. She had no interest in the other man. While she could recognise that the recruiter was good-looking and charming, she'd felt no spark of attraction.

In fact, those sparks—as Max had called them—had been few and far between. And they'd never been strong enough to make her want to be with someone else. Not while there was still a piece of paper that had gone unsigned for far too long.

Maybe it was time to confront the issue. 'Do you want to sign the divorce papers? Is that why I'm here?'

His gaze darkened, lips thinning slightly. 'I brought you here so you could see what I've been doing with myself for the past three years. If I remember right, you were the one who expressed an interest.'

The soft anger in his voice made her fingers clench on the pen. Okay, so maybe it had been rude to come out and ask, but the subject was like the elephant in the room that no one wanted to talk about.

And evidently, Max still didn't want to talk about it. Something in her heart became lighter, though, at the words. So he wasn't any more anxious than she was to finally close the chapter on their failed relationship.

But why?

Did she really want to sit here and dissect all

the possible reasons? Or was she simply going to take another sip of wine and go back to filling out the papers? She lifted the glass to her lips.

A few seconds went by, and then a warm hand touched her arm. 'Hey. I'm sorry. I didn't want to come here alone, and you were the person I chose to bring. Can't that be enough?'

Yes. It could.

She drew in a deep breath and let it out in a whisper of sound. 'I'm sorry. And I wanted to come too. So yes, let's just leave it at that for now, shall we?'

His fingers moved slowly down her arm, along her glove, until his hand covered hers on the table. 'Then as soon as you're finished with that form, will you dance with me?'

Letting her fingers circle his for a brief second, she lifted them with a nod. 'Yes. I'd love to.'

Max's hand slid around her waist and swung her around the room for a second time, the music pulling him into a world where nothing else ex-

isted but her touch and the synchronised move-
ments of their bodies as they danced together. It
had been ages since he'd held her like this.

It felt good and right, and he wasn't exactly
sure why. What he did know was that he didn't
want this night to end any time soon.

Maybe it didn't have to.

Annabelle had said she didn't want any expectations or any preconceived ideas.

Had she meant that she didn't want the past to
stand in the way of them being together tonight?
He had no idea. But if she was willing to just
take tonight as it came, then maybe he should
be okay with doing the same.

And with her cheek pressed against his left
shoulder, he wasn't in a hurry to do anything to
change the situation.

He'd been an idiot about Dale being there with
her at the table. But the man—a general physi-
cian—had somehow charmed his way into more
than one bed when they'd served on the medical
mission in Sudan that year. The women hadn't

complained, but back then Max had been too raw from his own heartache to take kindly to someone jumping from one person to the next.

He'd fielded some veiled invitations of his own from female volunteers, but he hadn't taken any of them up on their offers. In reality, he hadn't wanted anyone. The sting of rejection when Anna had asked him to leave had penetrated deep, leaving no room for anything else but work. In reality, he'd been happy to be alone. It was a condition he was well acquainted with.

And something he didn't want to think about right now.

'Are you okay?' He murmured the words into her hair, breathing deeply and wondering what the hell he was playing at.

'Mmm.'

It wasn't really an answer, but the sound made something come alive in his gut. How long had they been here, anyway?

Not that he wanted to look at his watch. In fact,

he didn't want to leave at all. But they couldn't stay here all night, and once they left...

It was over.

'Anna?'

'Yes?'

He paused, trying to figure out what he wanted. 'Are you still okay with spending the night in London?'

Her feet stopped moving for a second. 'Yes. I can stay with my folks if you don't want me at the flat, although I didn't ask Mum if she had room.'

'We can share the flat. I just wasn't sure if you'd decided you wanted to get back to Cheltenham—'

'No. As long as we can check on Hope at some point, I have no plans until my shift starts midday tomorrow.' She eased back to look into his face. 'Unless *you've* changed your mind.'

Not hardly.

But he should have told her he had. Because holding her brought back memories of dancing with her other times, when life was simpler and all that mattered was their love for each other. Seeing that picture on the wall at Anna's parents' house had made all those feelings come back in a rush. He'd been having trouble tamping them down again, but he'd better work out how.

Because, as of now, he and Anna were going to be sharing their flat one last night.

And the memories and feelings that haunted that place were a thousand times more powerful than anything he might have felt as he'd looked at that wall of pictures. His heart thudded heavy in his chest as the music changed, the singer they'd hired shifting to a lower octave, his voice throaty with desire. The mood in the place changed along with it, dancers beginning to hold each other a little closer.

Right on cue, the arms around his neck tightened just a hair, bringing his face closer to hers. And suddenly all he wanted to do was kiss her.

'Anna...'

Her eyes slowly came up and focused on his.

He saw the exact same longing in them that he felt in his gut. Tired to hell of fighting what he'd been wanting to do for days, Max lowered his head and pressed his lips to hers.

Nothing was fast enough.

Annabelle's body couldn't keep up with the ricochet of emotions as Max spun her back into his arms the second they were inside the lift at their old flat, heading towards the fourth floor. Thank heavens no one else was in the compartment, because it felt as if she were on fire, and the only one who could quench the blaze was having none of it. He was keeping the flames fanned to inferno-like proportions.

Her gloved fingers gripped the expensive fabric of his tuxedo jacket as she tried desperately to return kiss for kiss…to respond to his murmured words. In the end, all she could do was hang on and pray they reached the flat before the dam totally broke and the camera caught them doing something that could get them arrested.

Ping! Ping!

Finally. The soft sound signalled they had arrived at their destination. The only thing left was to… The doors opened.

'Max.' His name came out as half chuckle, half moan as she tried to tug him to the side. 'We need to get off.'

His fingers tunnelled into her hair, his lips nibbling on the line of her jaw and making her shiver with need. 'And if I don't want to move out of the lift?'

'Then…*ooh!*…then we're going to be stuck riding it for the rest of the night.'

'Bloody hell.' His pained smile put paid to his words, but he stuck a hand between the doors just as they were getting ready to close. 'The image of you "riding it for the rest of the night…"'

They slid into the foyer, a ring of doors lining the fourth floor. She tried to call to mind the number of their flat, but, with her head this fuzzy with need, she was having trouble. 'I don't—'

'Four-oh-three.'

Gripping her hand as if afraid she might try to flee before they made it inside, he came up with a set of keys from one of the pockets of his trousers.

No way. She wasn't about to run.

Somehow Max got the key fitted into the lock and turned it. They practically fell inside the door.

Home!

No, not home. But close enough.

Dumping the keys onto the marble table in the foyer, he navigated through a hallway, switching lights on as he went, towing her behind him. She glanced around as they went through the flat.

It was immaculate. He'd said that Suzanne came once a month to clean. Annabelle didn't even want to think about how much money that added up to over the course of the last couple of years.

The place looked just as she'd left it. Her mum had told her to take the furniture with her to her new flat, but Annabelle hadn't wanted anything to do with the sad remains of their marriage. So she'd just left it all for Max to dispose of. It looked as if he hadn't wanted to be left in charge of that task any more than she had.

Down the hallway, past a bathroom and two guest bedrooms, until they arrived at their old room. Three years later, the brown silk spread still adorned the bed, looking brand-new. It could have been a mausoleum preserving a slice of her life that had been both happy and filled with anguish.

'I can't believe it's all still here.'

That seemed to stop Max for a moment. He looked around as if seeing it all for the first time. 'I haven't been here in ages. I always meant to change things, but...'

He hadn't been able to any more than she had.

'Let's not think about that right now.' She wrapped her arms around his waist, unwilling to ruin what had been building between them ever since they'd come face to face in the corridors of Teddy's. It seemed as if every tick of the clock had been leading to this.

Whatever 'this' was.

He cupped her face in his hands. 'Let's not,' he agreed before moving in to kiss her once more.

Again and again, his lips touched hers until the fire was back and this time there was nothing to hold them back.

Annabelle pushed his tuxedo jacket from his shoulders, moving to catch it when it started to drop to the floor.

'Leave it.' His knuckles dragged up the length of her neck, smoothing along the line of her jaw until he reached her ear. He toyed with one of her chandelier earrings, making it swing on her lobe in a way that made her shudder. He'd always known exactly how to make her melt like a pot of jelly that had been exposed to a heat source.

And he was the ultimate heat source, his body generating temperatures that threatened to scorch her until nothing was left but smouldering embers.

And she was fine with that.

He reached around and found the zipper on her dress—began edging it downward.

'Wait!'

She wasn't sure quite why she said that word, other than the fact that she wasn't wearing a bra under the gown, and if he got her dress off— well, she would be standing there in only her underwear while Max was almost fully clothed.

He evidently misunderstood because he went very still. Too still.

'Max?'

'Do you want me to stop?' He leaned back to look at her face.

'Yes. I mean no.' She shook her head, trying to form her words in a way that wouldn't sound completely off the wall. 'I'm not wearing…um… anything under this. I was hoping to even up the odds a little bit first.'

'You're not wearing *anything*?' He took a step back and dragged a hand through his hair. 'I am very glad I didn't know that while we were out on the dance floor. Or driving over here. Or in the lift.'

'I'm not totally naked. There was just no way to wear a bra with the back of the dress the way it is.'

He moved in again, his fingers trailing up the length of her spine and then walking back down it. 'Very glad I didn't know that, either. But now that I do…' His fingers again reached for the zipper and tugged it down, while Annabelle scrambled to hold up the front of her dress.

'What happened to evening up the odds?'

'I kind of like the odds the way they are.'

'You mean when they're in your favour?'

Max grinned at her but took a step back and began undoing the knot of his bow tie. 'You want even? You've got it.'

Not fair!

'But I wanted to do that.'

'It's much safer this way.' He pulled the tie through the starched white collar of his shirt and let it drop on top of his jacket.

'Safer for whom?'

'For me. And for you.' His fingers went to the first button of the shirt.

This time she groaned. Then a thought came to her. He'd done this on purpose. If she was holding up the front of her dress, she wouldn't be able to touch him, which meant…

That the thought of her doing so was making him as crazy as he was making her.

Well, two can play at that game, Max Ainsley!

'Oh, Max…' She let his name play over her tongue.

His hands stopped where they were, his brows coming together.

With what she hoped was a saucy smile, she let go of her dress, glad when it whispered down her body and pooled at her feet, instead of just staying put and forcing her to awkwardly push it to the ground.

His reaction was more than worth it. A blast of profanity-laced air hissed from his mouth as he stood there and stared. And when she started to move a step forward, he lurched backwards.

Annabelle was glad she'd decided to wear her laciest underwear ever, the red matching her dress to a tee. They rode high up on her hips and, while not quite a thong, they'd been advertised as Brazilian cut, which meant there was only a narrow band of fabric that covered her behind.

She peeled one of her gloves off in a long smooth move, and then the other, letting each of them land on top of her dress. 'Now the odds are even, don't you think?' She moved forward again, and this time Max stayed put. Maybe he was just incapable of thought right now, which had been her exact intent. She pressed her palms against his chest, gratified to feel the pounding of his heart beneath her touch. 'Let me help you with those buttons, since you seem to be having trouble.'

He still didn't say anything as she somehow managed to flip open one white button after another, until she reached the one at the top of his cummerbund. Pressing herself against his chest and gratified to hear yet another gust of air above her head, she reached around him to find the fastening at the back that held the wide satin band in place. It too hit the floor.

Evidently, Max had had all he could take, because his hands wrapped around her upper arms and eased her away from him. 'You're a witch, you know that?'

'Mmm-hmm. Be careful, or I might cast an evil spell on you.'

'A spell? Yes. I think you already have.' He swooped her up into his arms and dumped her in the middle of the bed, the brown silk rippling out from her landing spot. 'Although whether it's evil or not is yet to be seen.'

Max backed up several paces and made short work of the rest of his buttons, undoing the fastening on the front of his black trousers. And this time it was Annabelle who got to enjoy the show, as his strong chest appeared along with those taut abs. Off came his shoes and black socks.

The man made her mouth water. Even his feet were sexy.

Then he hesitated, and her attention shot back to his face.

'What are you doing?'

His smile this time was a bit forced, the lopsided gesture she loved so much tipped a little lower than normal. 'I'm trying to hold it together.'

Annabelle's relieved sigh was full of pure joy. He wasn't having second thoughts. He wanted this just as much as she did. 'Then why don't you come over here and let me hold it for a while?'

'Did I call you a witch yet?' His laughter came out sounding choked, but at least his voice had lost that weird edge he'd had moments earlier.

'Yes.' She leaned up on one elbow and crooked a finger at him. 'Time to stop stalling and let me help you finish.'

'That's exactly what I'm afraid of, Anna: that you'll help me finish before I'm ready.'

'Hmm…we can take care of that on the next round.'

'Next?' He came forward until he was close enough for her to go into action. She sat up and scooted her butt to the edge of the bed until he stood between her thighs.

'Yes, next.' She said the word with conviction, reaching again for his waistband. This time the zipper went down, and he made no effort to stop her. Pushing his trousers down his legs, she let him kick them out of the way. 'And now, Maxwell Ainsley, we're finally even.'

They both still had their underwear on.

'You first, then.' Max leaned over her, planting his hands on the bed on either side of her thighs, but he made no effort to strip her bare. Instead, his lips found hers, his touch soft and sweet and somehow just as erotic as the more demanding kisses had been. She tipped her head up, absorbing each tiny taste, each brush of friction as they came together over and over. Soon, though, the V between her parted legs began to send up a protest, a needy throbbing making itself known. She pushed herself even closer to the edge of the bed, her thighs spreading further. It didn't help.

Well, his 'you first' might mean she was supposed to strip him first, right? So that was exactly what she would do. Hooking her thumbs in the elastic band on his hips, she gave a quick tug before he could say or do anything, pushing them down to his knees.

'Cheater,' he murmured, not moving from his spot, every syllable causing his lips to brush against hers.

'We never set any ground rules, if I remember right. And if you'll just stand up, I'll finish the job.'

'I don't trust you.'

'No?' She gave him a smile full of meaning. 'Well, there's more than one way to skin a cat... or undress a man.'

With that she lay back on the bed, kicked off her high-heeled pumps and slid her bare feet up the backs of his calves. When she reached the spot where his boxers were still clinging to his legs, she pushed them as far down as she could. Max still hadn't moved a muscle…except for the one currently ticking away on the side of his jaw.

What she didn't expect was for his hands to whisk up her sides and cover her breasts, the warm heat and promise of his touch making the nipples harden instantly. He didn't stay there, however; his fingers were soon travelling down the line of her belly until he reached her own underwear and dragged them down her thighs, moving backwards as he inched them over her legs, across her ankles and finally pulled them free of her body. He stepped out of his boxers while he was at it. Or at least she assumed he did, since she couldn't actually see him do it.

This time when he parted her legs, there was no mistaking his intent.

'You want to play with fire, Anna? Well, you've got it.'

With that, he put his hands beneath her bottom and tugged. Hard. Hard enough that she slid forward to meet his ready flesh. 'Is this what you want?'

The part of her that had been throbbing in anticipation clenched, thinking he was going to give it to her right away. Instead, he slid up past it, eliciting a whispered complaint from her. It ended in a moan when he found that nerve-rich area just a little higher.

He repeated the act. Words failed her, a jumble of sensations eclipsing her ability to think, much less talk.

Her eyes fluttered closed, the release she'd sought just seconds ago now rushing at her much too quickly.

His voice came from above her. 'I think it is.'

His fingertips found her nipples once again and squeezed, the dual assault wracking her body with a pleasure so sharp it made her arch up seeking him. 'Max.'

He gave her what she wanted then, thrusting

forward and finding her immediately. The movement was so sudden it made her gasp, her fingers clutching his shoulders as he set up a quick rhythm that didn't give her any room to catch her breath. Instead it tossed her high into the air and held her there for several seconds, and then she was over the edge, her body spasming around his. Max groaned, his mouth finding hers as he plunged again and again before finally slowing, the sound of his heavy breathing wonderfully loud in her ears.

She wrapped her arms around his neck, holding him tight as the emotions she'd been holding back finally bubbled over, tears slipping silently down her cheeks. Annabelle came to a stunning realisation.

She loved her husband.

She didn't just *love* him. She was *in* love with him. She'd never stopped being in love with him. She'd submerged the truth—buried it far out of sight—and tried to lose herself in caring for sick children instead. Only it hadn't worked. Not entirely.

Because here it was. In plain sight.

Annabelle loved him. Deeply. Entirely. And she had no idea what she was going to do about it.

CHAPTER NINE

IT HADN'T FELT like goodbye sex.

The deep sleep that had finally pulled Max under in the early hours of the morning released him just as quickly.

He blinked a couple of times, trying to bring to mind exactly what had happened last night, but it all blurred together to form a scene of decadence and exhausting satisfaction.

Annabelle.

He turned his head to look at her side of the bed only to find it empty—the nightstand bare of anything except a clock. No note. He frowned before remembering that they'd come to London together, so it wasn't likely that she'd slipped out and caught a train back to Cheltenham. So she was still here. Somewhere.

She was here.

He relaxed and rolled onto his back, settling into the pillows with his hands behind his head. It was just seven in the morning. They might even have time for another session before they had to be on their way.

And do what afterwards?

He wasn't sure. But maybe they could start again. In the crush of timetables and thermometers and ovulation charts, Max had forgotten just how good sex—real sex, not something with a goal in mind—had been between them. Last night had brought it all rushing back. Their first year had been out of this world. They'd been so in tune with each other's needs that it had seemed nothing would be able to come between them.

Until it had.

Maybe they could get back to the 'before' part of the equation.

Was he actually thinking of getting back together with her? Could they erase what had torn them apart and start over? If so, they could just put off signing any papers for a while and wander down this lane for a few miles and see what happened.

Unless Annabelle didn't want to do that.

Didn't someone say that couples who were getting divorced would sometimes fall into each other's arms one last time as a way of saying goodbye or having closure? What they'd done hadn't seemed like that. At least not to him.

Vaguely he was aware of the sound of running water. Ah, that answered the question as to where she was. She was taking a shower.

Naked.

She probably had soap streaming down her body.

Naked.

When the word popped up a second time, he smiled. Hadn't he just thought about how it was still early?

Well, they could kill two birds with one stone. He could soap her back, while doing a few other things.

Throwing the blankets off, he realised the flat was chilly. The heat must be turned down, since Suzanne hadn't expected anyone to be living here.

He'd have to call her this morning and let her know he'd spent the night so she didn't come into the flat, realise someone had been in there and assume there'd been an intruder. And he'd promised he would call the hospital first thing to see how Baby Hope was doing. This was a good time to do that.

Bringing up the number on his smartphone, he rang the main desk of the hospital.

'This is Mr Ainsley. Is Miss McDonald in yet?'

'Let me check.'

The voice clicked off and became elevator music as he was put on hold. The shower was still running. Even if she came out before he was done with his call, he would just coax her back under the spray.

The music stopped and Sienna's voice came over the line. 'Hi, Max. Everything okay?'

It was more than okay, but that wasn't something he was going to tell anyone. Not yet.

'Fine. I'm just checking on our patient.'

He could practically hear a smile form on the other doctor's lips. 'We have several patients. Which one are you referring to?'

This time the smile was on his end. 'A certain young transplant patient.'

'She's fine. No more episodes of a-fib.' There was a pause. 'I do seem to remember telling you I would call you if there was any change.'

'You did. But I wanted to be able to tell…' This time it was Max who stopped short. He wasn't really ready for anyone to know that he and Annabelle had spent the night together. 'I just wanted to see if I needed to rush back this morning or not.'

'No need to rush at all. She's doing brilliantly.'

'Good. Thank you for taking over her case during my absence.'

'Not a problem at all. Are you coming back today?'

'Yes.' Which brought back to mind what he'd set out to do when he got out of bed. 'I'll be in around four o'clock this afternoon. Call me if you need me.'

'I will. Have a safe trip.'

'Thank you.'

Max rang off, scrubbing a hand through his hair. And now back to his previous thoughts of Annabelle and that shower.

Before he headed for the bathroom, though, he made a quick detour down the hallway and turned the heating up to a tolerable level—the amazing thing was they hadn't noticed the cold last night when they'd been making love. Then he padded back to the bathroom, stopping just outside the door.

The shower was definitely running.

He hadn't put on any clothes before falling asleep so that saved him a step. His mouth watered. He could certainly use a shower. Now more than ever.

Trying the doorknob and finding it unlocked,

he eased into the room. Steam enveloped the space. She'd been in here a while. But then again, he remembered Annabelle had loved long, luxurious baths and showers. Her skin would be soft and moist...

Gulping, he removed his watch and placed it on the counter and then turned towards the shower enclosure. He could just barely make out Annabelle's form through the frosted glass. His body hardened all over again. How did she do that to him?

It was almost as if they'd been given a clean slate. Something he'd needed—they'd both needed.

With that thought in his head, he wrapped a hand around the handle of the door just as the water switched off.

Damn!

Yanking the door open, he found a pink-faced Annabelle, her hair streaming down her back, eyes wide with surprise.

'Max! I thought you were still asleep.'

'I was. But then I heard the shower and thought I might take one too.'

Her slow smile lit up the enclosure. 'I think I might have left you a little hot water. If you can be quick.'

'Did you forget? We had an on-demand unit put in. I can be as slow as I want to be.'

'Can you?' Her smile widened. 'I may have missed a spot or two, then. Do you mind if I join you?'

'I was counting on it.'

With that, Max closed the door and turned on the shower. Then, with the sting of hot water pelting his back, he put everything else out of his mind as he moved to turn on Anna.

Annabelle stretched up to kiss Max's shoulder one last time, her body warm and limp as she stood on the warm tiles of the shower enclosure. 'Were you able to call the hospital yet?'

'How did I know you were going to ask that?' He gathered her hair in his hand and squeezed the excess water out. 'I've missed doing this.'

'Showering?'

'Showering…with you.'

'I've missed it too. Along with…' Her hands swept down his chest, heading to regions below, only to have him catch her before she reached her destination.

'Witch. Is that all you've missed?'

Was there a hint of insecurity in that voice? Impossible. Max was never insecure. He always knew exactly what he wanted. Or didn't want.

A chill went over her.

No. He'd said he'd missed her. Or had he? Hadn't his exact words been that he'd missed showering with her? Having sex with her?

Not exactly. He'd stopped her from stroking him. Had asked if that was all she'd missed. Maybe he was seeking reassurance.

'No, it's not all I've missed. I've missed…us.' She tried to let the sincerity in her voice ring through.

Threading his fingers through hers, he nodded. 'So have I. And yes, I called the hospital. Hope is doing fine.'

'Thank God. Maybe this will be a happy Christmas after all.' She wasn't above seeking a little reassurance herself.

'I'm hoping it will.' Letting her go, he stepped out of the shower, leaving her alone. Just when the worry centres began firing in her head, he came back, a thick white towel in his hands. Another one was wrapped around his waist.

'I guess this means fun time is over?'

'Didn't you say you had a shift this afternoon?'

'Oh! That's right.' How could she have forgotten that? Maybe because when Max was around, she tended to forget everything.

When she went to grab the towel from him, he held it just out of reach. 'Not so fast. There's something else I've missed.'

With that, he opened the fluffy terry and proceeded to pat her dry, starting with her face and gently moving down her body, until he was kneeling before her, sweeping the towel down her thighs and calves. A familiar tingling began stirring in her midsection. 'You'd better be careful, or I'm never going to let you out of this room.'

'I can think of worse things than being kept as your prisoner.'

The towel moved between her legs, teasing more intimate territory.

A low moan came from her throat before she could stop it. 'That's so not fair. You didn't let me touch you.'

His eyes came up to meet hers. 'You have more control than I do.'

'Wanna bet?' She tangled her fingers in his hair, letting the warm moist strands filter between them. 'I've never been able to resist you. I really do need to get to work, though.'

He stood. 'See? More control. Bend over.'

'Wh…what?' The word sputtered out on a half-laugh.

'Naughty girl. Not for that.' He grinned, the act taking years off his face. 'Now bend over.'

She did as he asked, and Max flipped her hair over until the strands hung straight down. Then he wrapped the towel around her head and twisted it, enveloping her wet locks in it. A glimmer of disappointment went through her. Max had it all wrong. She had no control when it came to him. She wanted him. All the time.

And now that things seemed to be easing between them, maybe she'd be able to have him whenever she wanted him. At least that was what she hoped. Surely he felt the same way as she did.

She tightened the towel and then stood upright again, letting the end of it slide down the back of her head. Luckily there was still a hairdryer in the flat. She'd found it when searching through the drawers.

Max opened the shower door for her and let her step out. A wave of steam followed her as he wrapped her in a second towel. 'Good thing we don't have an alarm that is triggered by heat.'

'Yes, that's a very good thing.' He encircled

her waist and pulled her back against him. 'I can think of several times during the night when we might have set it off, if so.'

'I can think of several times that you went off too.'

He dropped a kiss on her hair, and she felt something stir against her backside. He gave a strangled laugh. 'Maybe we'd better not talk about that right now.'

Maybe they shouldn't. Because the tingling that had started when he'd towel-dried her was getting stronger. 'Okay, let me get dressed and dry my hair, and I'll be ready.'

He tipped up her head and gave her a soft kiss. 'Okay, but it's under duress.' Letting her go, he dragged his hands through his own wet hair, which settled right into place.

'That is so not fair. You don't have to do anything to look great.'

'Neither do you.' He tapped her nose with his finger. 'You are perfect just as you are.'

'I don't know about that, but I do feel perfectly

satisfied.' She went over and opened a drawer, finding the hairdryer she'd discovered earlier. She picked it up, laughing as a thought hit her. 'After all those contortions we did years ago, wouldn't it be funny if last night or this morning did what all the hormone treatments couldn't? So…do you want a boy or a girl?'

It was only when she picked up her hairbrush that she realised Max wasn't laughing. He had gone very still.

He slipped his watch around his wrist, before looking up. His eyes were completely blank, although a muscle ticked in his jaw. 'A boy or a girl?'

A sliver of alarm went through her at the slow words. Where was the man who had just made love to her as if he couldn't get enough?

She forced a smile to her face. One she didn't feel. 'It's just that it would be ironic, if I got pregnant when we weren't even trying.'

Actually, it wouldn't be funny. Or ironic. Or anything else. Why had she even said that?

Max turned and went into the bedroom. With a panicked sense of déjà vu, Annabelle followed him, finding the bed was perfectly made. So perfectly that if she hadn't remembered writhing like a maniac beneath those sheets, she might have thought it was all a dream.

Only that exquisite bit of soreness in all the right places said it had been very real.

Except there was that weird vibe she'd picked up after joking about getting pregnant. He hadn't looked or sounded like someone who would be thrilled about that happening. Maybe she should put his mind at ease. She moved closer.

'Hey, are you afraid I might get pregnant because of what we did?'

His pupils darkened, expanding until they seemed to take up his entire iris. 'I think the more appropriate question would be: are you afraid you *won't* get pregnant?'

She blinked. 'No, of course not. I was joking.'

'Were you? Because right now, I don't feel like laughing.'

Neither did she. She had no idea why the pregnancy thing had crossed her mind. Maybe because it had been so long since they'd had sex that was totally spontaneous.

Nothing like bringing up a whole slew of bad memories, though.

He turned away and picked up his overnight bag, setting it on the bed.

Annabelle caught at his arm, forcing him to face her again. 'Look, I'm sorry. Obviously it's still a touchy subject.'

'Touchy would be an understatement.' The thin line of his mouth was a warning she remembered from days past. 'Is this why you were so eager to get back to the flat last night—were you trying to hit a certain magic window? If so, you've got the wrong man.'

'I wasn't doing anything of the sort! You're being ridiculous.'

It was as if everything they'd done last night had been swept away, dropping them back into the same angry arguments from their past.

'I'm being ridiculous?' His tone was dangerously soft. 'Funny you should say that, because I seem to remember a whole lot of ridiculousness that went on during our marriage. That journal you kept being one of them.'

The words slapped at Annabelle, leaving her speechless for several seconds. He considered their attempts to have a baby 'ridiculousness'?

The pain in her gut and the throbbing in her chest were duelling with each other, seeking the nearest available exit: her eyes. But she couldn't let the gathering tears stop her from trying one last time.

'Max, I wasn't serious about what I said in the bathroom.'

It was as if he hadn't heard her at all. 'We should have used some kind of protection. I meant what I said three years ago. I don't want children.'

His words stopped her all over again.

'Ever?'

'Ever. I thought I made that perfectly clear.'

He had. But that had been three years ago. A lot had changed since then. Maybe more than she'd thought. He'd never once mentioned still loving her. Not last night. Not this morning. The closest he'd come was the word 'spark'.

Oh, God, how could she have been so stupid? And just to prove that she was, the words kept pouring out.

'I don't understand what you're saying.'

'No? I'm saying this was a mistake, Annabelle.' He glanced one last time at the open bag on the bed. 'When we get back to Cheltenham, I'm going to find those divorce papers and sign them.' There was a long pause, and she suddenly knew the hammer was going to fall and crush her beneath its blow. 'And if you haven't already, I'm going to ask that you sign them too.'

'Please don't say that, Max. Let's talk about it.'

'There is nothing to talk about. You wanted a divorce? Well, guess what, honey, so do I.'

CHAPTER TEN

THE TRIP BACK to Cheltenham had been made in total silence. She could have tried to plead her case, but she doubted that Max would have heard anything she had to say.

Just as in their marriage, he had shut down emotionally. His face and the tight way he'd gripped the wheel had seemed to confirm that, so Annabelle had stared out of the window at the passing countryside, doing her best not to burst into tears.

He wasn't any more willing to fight for her—for *them*—than he had been three years ago. And she was done trying.

She loved him, but she was not going to kneel at his feet and beg him not to leave.

After working her afternoon shift—during which she hadn't seen Max a single time, not even to check on Hope—she'd spent a long sleepless night, first in her bed, and when that hadn't worked she'd lain on the sofa.

This morning, she was exhausted, but resigned. If he wanted to sign the papers, she was going to let him. She unpacked her bag, staring at herself in the mirror for a long time.

Was he right? Had some subconscious part hoped she might become pregnant because of what they'd done? Maybe. And if she was honest with herself, there was probably some long-lost side of her that would always harbour a tiny sliver of hope. How could she just extinguish it?

She couldn't. And evidently Max would not be able to love the side of her that wanted children.

Okay. She would just deal with it, as she had the last time.

She went to the shelf and picked up the manila envelope, blowing three years' worth of dust off it. Sitting at her desk, she withdrew the papers inside, her hand shaking as she laid them out flat, realising she'd never really looked at what her solicitor had sent over. Max wasn't the only one who had put off walking this through to the end.

Petition for dissolution of the
marriage between
Maxwell Wilson Ainsley
and
Annabelle Brookes Ainsley

She was listed as the petitioner and he was the respondent. In other words, she was asking for the divorce and it was up to Max to respond.

Which he had, yesterday.

The night before last she'd felt such hope. And now here she was, back where she'd started three years ago.

Only worse. Because back then, when he'd issued his ultimatum about discontinuing the IVF attempts, she hadn't completely believed him. Until she'd caught him looking at that ovulation journal. She'd seen his face and had known it was over.

But that was all in the past. At least she'd

thought so until yesterday. She'd had no idea he harboured such terrible resentment of their time together.

After they'd made love, Annabelle could have sworn that those old hurts had been healed. Obviously she'd been wrong.

Annabelle stared at the document.

She was the petitioner.

The word swirled through her mind again and again. Just because someone asked for something didn't mean the other person had to give it to them, did it? No, but Max seemed more than willing to let her have what she wanted. Only she wasn't sure she wanted it any more.

Why? Because he'd hurt her pride? No. That hurt went far deeper than that.

What if she, the petitioner, *withdrew* her request? Was that even possible? She could try to stop the process and, if Max insisted, let it turn into a long drawn-out battle in the courts. She could try to hurt him the way he'd hurt her. But that wasn't what Annabelle wanted. She didn't want to hurt him. Or to fight with him.

She didn't want to fight at all.

But that didn't mean that wasn't what should happen.

Hadn't her parents always taught her to fight for what she believed in? And wasn't that what she'd expected of Max all those years ago?

Yes.

Even now, despite his angry words, she believed they had a chance if they let go of the past. But did Max believe the same thing? After yesterday, she wasn't sure.

Why had he got so angry after she'd joked about her getting pregnant?

Because he thought she still wanted children and he didn't?

That was what he'd implied when he'd mentioned hitting the 'magic' window: *If so, you've got the wrong man.*

She didn't know for sure, because Max had *refused to talk to her*!

So, she had a choice. Let him sign and be done with it. Or go and have it out with him. Whether he wanted to or not.

Where? She had no idea if he'd even gone in to work yesterday afternoon.

She could always go to his house. If she knew where that was. She realised she didn't have a clue where he lived.

But she knew someone who did.

Max circled his living room for what seemed like the hundredth time, trying to find some kind of peace with his decision. If he could leave the country, as he had three years ago, he would. But he had a contract to fulfil, and he was dead tired of running.

He loved Annabelle. More than life itself.

But the thought of standing by a second time while she destroyed her health and more over a dream that was never going to come true was a knife to the heart. That time she'd retained fluid and had been so sick, he'd been afraid he was going to lose her. It had all turned into one huge ball of misery. The empty promises from fertility doctors. The tears. The torment. There had been no holy grail. No miracle.

And when she'd finally realised he was serious that last time? She'd told him to leave. Had sent him packing, cutting him off from the only real and good thing he'd ever known. And he'd been willing to walk away to make it all stop.

His statement about there being no miracle wasn't entirely true. There had been. But it hadn't been in what he or any of the doctors could give to Anna. It was what Anna had given to him: a love like none he'd ever known.

And what had he done? He'd thrown it away a second time. Because he'd been afraid.

Could he undo the things he'd said? Maybe, but how did he convince her to be happy with what she had? With him?

A cold hand clutched his chest. Was that what it had been? Had he been jealous of her attempts to have a child?

No. He could answer that honestly. That wasn't his reason for walking out on her yesterday. And yes, even though he hadn't physically left the vicinity, he had walked away from the burgeoning hope of a new beginning.

And for what?

For a few careless words uttered in a bathroom? Had he really stopped to listen to what she was saying, or had he simply assumed she was headed down the same old path?

The problem was, he hadn't actually heard her out, he'd simply blurted out that he didn't want children and that he wanted to finalise the divorce.

Was she waiting for him to sign the papers? Was she even now informing her solicitor to finish what she'd started?

His throat tightened until it was difficult to breathe. She should. She should leave him far behind and forget all about him.

But he didn't want her to.

So what should he do?

Probably what he should have done three years ago. Stand in front of her and listen to her heart, rather than issue ultimatums. Hear what it was she wanted out of life. If it came out that they wanted completely different things, then he could walk away with no regrets. It was just that Max wasn't so sure they did. They had worked together—had loved together—in a way that had made him hope that this time might be the charm.

Weren't those almost the exact same words that Annabelle had said in that bathroom?

Yes.

So why was he standing here wondering if he'd done the right thing? He needed to find her and pray that he wasn't too late.

Opening his wardrobe, he grabbed a leather jacket and headed towards the front door. He could always camp in front of Baby Hope's hospital room and wait for Annabelle to show up. Because if he knew one thing about the woman it was that she loved that baby. She had fought for the infant's survival time after time. Maybe it was time that someone—him—decided to fight for Annabelle.

Just as he reached for the doorknob his bell rang, startling the hell out of him.

He frowned. *Come on. I really need a break here.*

Wrenching the door open to tell whoever it was that he didn't have time for chit-chat, he was shocked to find the person he'd just been thinking about standing on his front mat.

No. That couldn't be right.

He forced his gaze to pull the image into sharp focus. Still the same.

'Anna?' Her eyes looked red, and she carried a packet under her arm. 'Are you okay?'

'No. No, I'm not, actually.' She took a deep breath and then held up an envelope. 'But I brought my copy of the divorce papers. If you have yours, you can sign them, and I'll take them both to my solicitor.'

His throat clogged with emotion. He was too late. He'd brought the axe down on something that could have made him happy for the rest of his life. He should tell her he wasn't going to sign them, that it wasn't what he wanted at all, but somehow the words wouldn't form.

Because she was going to leave him all over again.

It's not like you didn't tell her to.

'Are you going to ask me in?'

Realising she was standing in the cold, he took a step back, motioning her inside his cottage.

'Let me take your coat and hat.'

Annabelle shed both items, handing the gear to him, but retaining her hold of the envelope. 'Thank you.'

He led her into the living room and made her a cup of tea, while she perched on the couch, the packet resting across the knees of her jeans. He wanted to take it from her and toss it into the gas fireplace he'd switched on, but hadn't he decided to listen to her heart? To hear her out without jumping to any conclusions?

But she said he could sign his copy of the papers right there in front of her.

If he wanted to.

He waited until she'd had her second sip of tea before wading into the waters. 'You didn't have to bring your copy. I have one of my own.'

He couldn't imagine saying anything more stupid than that.

'I know. But I wanted to come by and get a few things off my chest. In person.'

Taking a gulp of his coffee and feeling the scald as it went down his throat, he paused to let her talk.

Reaching deep into her handbag, she pulled out a notebook. Max recognised the green floral cover and immediately stiffened. Why did she even still have that?

'When I was packing my things to come to Cheltenham, I found this, and realised the enormity of the mistake I'd made all those years ago. Keeping this a secret was wrong on so many levels.' Her chest rose as she took a deep breath. 'What I said in the bathroom had nothing to do with this. I meant the words as a joke, but they backfired horribly and ended up shooting me in the heart. I wasn't scheming to get pregnant after the fundraising party, I swear.'

'I'm just beginning to realise that.' One side of his mouth tilted slightly. 'I think you used the word "ridiculous" to describe my reaction. You were right.'

Her eyes searched his. 'I never should have said that. And just so you understand, I know I'm not going to get pregnant from having sex with you. Not two days ago. Not three months from now. Not ten years from now. I'm sorry if you thought that was what I was after. I'm not. Not any more.'

A pinpoint of hope appeared on the horizon. 'So you're not interested in having a baby?'

'If it happened, I would be ecstatic. But I'm not going to chase after it ever again. Especially knowing you don't want kids.'

'I never said that.' Even as the words came out, he realised he had. He'd said that very thing. Maybe he wasn't the only one who'd misunderstood. 'Okay, I did. But I meant I didn't want to go through the procedures any more. It hurt too much to see how they ripped you apart emotionally. Physically. Especially after that last attempt.'

He swallowed hard, forcing the words out. 'I thought you were going to die, Anna. And in the end, that's why I agreed to leave.'

'What?' The shock on her face was unmistakable.

He nodded. 'I've never done anything harder than walk through that door. The only thing that kept my feet moving was the thought that I might be saving your life. With me gone, you'd have no reason to go through any more treatments.'

'I—I never knew.'

If he'd been hoping she'd leap into his arms after that revelation, he was mistaken. Instead, she looked down at the journal in her hands, smoothing her fingers over the embossed cover. 'You hurt me, Max, when you came into that bathroom all those years ago and issued an edict that it was over. That I wasn't to try to get pregnant any more. I felt I had no control over anything, not even my own decisions.'

He knew he'd hurt her. 'You're right. We should have discussed it together.' He stood and walked towards a bank of windows that overlooked a park, stuffing his hands into his front pockets. 'It's just that seeing you in such torment... Well, it ripped my heart out.'

'And it killed me that I couldn't give you what you wanted.'

'What *I* wanted?' He turned back towards her.

'A family. You used to talk about how you wanted a big family, just like mine. So you could give our children what your parents hadn't given to you. And I wanted so desperately for you to have that. Then, when it came down to it—' her voice cracked '—I couldn't give it to you.'

He sat down next to her on the couch, horrified by her words. Had she really thought that? 'Anna, *you* were my family. Yes, I was disappointed that you couldn't get pregnant. But only because it seemed to be something you wanted so desperately.'

'I wanted it because of you.'

Could it be? Had he misread the signs all those years ago? Had he been so focused on the fights that had swirled around her efforts at conceiving that he'd missed the real reason she'd been so anguished after each failed attempt?

'I had no idea.' He took one of her hands.

'I asked you to leave because I was hurt and

trying to protect myself the only way I knew how. I took the coward's way out.'

'You're not a coward.' He took the journal from her, his thumb rubbing the edges of the little book. 'I am. Because I love you too much to watch you go through this again.'

'You love me?'

He stared at her. 'You didn't know?'

'I thought I did. At one time. But now?' She swallowed. 'I'm not sure.'

He set the journal on the coffee table and caught her face in his hands. 'I'm so sorry, Anna. Hell, I…' He bowed his head, trying to control the stinging in his eyes. Then he looked back up at her. 'I screwed everything up back then. And I screwed it up again at the flat yesterday morning.'

'So you don't want a divorce?'

He had to tread carefully. He wanted there to be no more misunderstandings. 'I don't. But I have to be sure of what you want out of life.'

'You aren't the only one who screwed up, Max. I wanted so badly to give you the things you didn't get as a child: roots and a huge amount of love.'

'You gave me those when you married me. That, along with your amazing, crazy family.'

'They all love you, you know. It's one of the reasons I couldn't bring myself to tell them about the divorce.' His eyes weren't the only ones stinging, evidently, judging from the moisture that appeared in hers. 'So where do we go from here?'

He thought for a minute.

'Maybe we should look at counselling. Find out how to handle everything we've been through. And after that?' He picked up her left hand and kissed the empty ring finger. 'I'd love to put something back on this.'

'I still have my rings.' She smiled. 'I don't think I've ever quite given up on us. It's why I never asked my solicitor to find you and demand those signed papers back. I think I was hoping that one day you would find your way home. And you did.'

He smiled back, linking his fingers with

hers. 'It would seem we have fate—and Sienna McDonald—to thank for that. Although I would like to think I would have come to my senses if your solicitor ever *had* hunted me down.'

She leaned her head on his shoulder. 'I guess I should have sicced him on you sooner, then.'

'Maybe you should have.' He dropped a kiss on her temple. 'I have to tell you that picture of us in your parents' dining room brought back memories of how happy we were. Of how things could have been had not things got so...'

'Insane.' She finished the sentence for him.

'I don't mean that in a bad way.'

'I know. But it was.' She lifted her head and motioned to the packet. 'That brings me back to my original question. Do you want me to hold onto these just in case it doesn't work out?'

'No.' Max got up from his seat and went over to a cabinet under his television. Opening the door, he retrieved an envelope that looked identical to hers. He sat back down, but didn't take the papers out. Instead, he folded the packet in half, trapping the journal in between. 'May I?'

He held out a hand for her envelope. When she gave it to him, he opened the flap and dropped the other items inside. Then he got up from the sofa. 'What I really want to do is toss these into the fireplace and watch them burn to ashes, but, since it's a gas fireplace, I'm afraid I'd set the cottage on fire.'

'That wouldn't be good.'

'No, it wouldn't. Especially since I'm hoping to move out of it very soon. I might not get my security deposit back.'

'Y-you're moving?' The fear on her face was enough to make him pull her from the sofa and enfold her in his arms.

'I'm sorry. I didn't mean I was moving away. I'm just hoping to change locations.'

'I don't understand.'

'Well, it might seem a little odd to your family and everyone at the hospital if you put your rings on and we continue living in separate homes, don't you think?'

Wrapping her arms around his neck, she pressed herself against him. 'Yes. It would. If you're thinking of coming to live at my place, I have to warn you that it's not as fancy as our flat in London, and—'

'It will be perfect, Anna. Just like you.'

With that he led her into the kitchen and stopped in front of the rubbish bin. Pushing the foot pedal, he waited until the top lifted all the way up. 'It's not as impressive as sending them up in a puff of smoke, but it'll be just as permanent. Once this lid falls, I don't want to mention these papers ever again.'

'Deal. But let's both do it.' She held one side of the envelope, while Max kept hold of the other end. Then they dropped it, along with all the hurts from the past, right where they belonged. Where they could never again poison their relationship.

Max released the pedal and let the lid drop back into place. 'Maybe in a couple of years we could move back to London. Or talk about adoption.'

'Adoption? You'd be okay with that?'

'As long as you are. I know with your sister—'

'I'm definitely open to that option.' She squeezed his hand. 'You might even be able to talk me into going on a medical mission, just like we used to dream about.'

'Are you serious?'

'Yes. I want to see what you've seen. Walk where you've walked. And I know that, this time, we'll be right in step with each other.'

He turned her until she faced him. 'I would be honoured to work alongside you, Mrs Ainsley.'

'And I, you.'

'How long before you have to be at Teddy's?'

She glanced at her watch. 'I have about two hours. I wasn't sure how long this was going to take or what state I would be in by the end of it.'

'Hmm... I think I might be able to answer both of those questions.' He gripped her hand and started leading her through the living room. 'This will take just about two hours...or however long you have left. And as for the state you'll be in by the end of it—I'm hoping you'll be in a state of undress and that you'll be very, very satisfied.'

'That sounds wonderful.' She caught up with him and put her arm around his waist. 'As for the satisfied part, I can't think of how I could be any more satisfied than I am at this very moment.'

They went through the bedroom door and he pushed it shut behind them. 'In that case, I plan to keep you that way for the rest of your life.'

EPILOGUE

ON EITHER SIDE of her, a small hand clutched hers as she walked slowly towards the waiting plane. After a ton of paperwork and countless trips to their solicitor's office, Annabelle and Max finally had their answer. Two boys with special needs were on their way to a brand-new life on a brand-new continent. Ready to join their sister, who was being cared for by Annabelle's mum.

Six months after Hope's surgery, the baby had come home to live with Annabelle and Max. The same solicitor who had handled this adoption had done a bit of digging and found a similar case where a preemie baby had been adopted by her nurse. It was enough to convince the courts that Hope belonged with them. Now two years old, she was growing and thriving and had brought such joy into their lives.

She glanced to the side where Max was making the final arrangements for the flight back to England. He stood tall and proud, no sign of the angry, frustrated man who'd walked out of her door all those years ago. And Annabelle had finally made her peace with never having a biological child. If it happened, it happened.

They'd compromised on that front. Max had agreed to not using birth control—with a sexy smile as they'd lain in bed after making love one night—and she'd agreed not to seek extraordinary means to have a child.

The life they now had was enough. More than enough.

Max meant the world to her. As did Hope, who had given them the best Christmas gift of all: a chance to rekindle their romance and to fix what was broken between them.

And now these two small gifts had come into their lives, both with heart defects that had needed surgery. Max and Annabelle had met

Omar and Ahmed on a brief Doctors Without Borders trip they'd made four months earlier. A colleague of Max's had performed the surgeries and Annabelle had fallen in love. With those two boys, and with Max all over again. His selfless need to help ease the suffering of others had been more than evident. Then and now.

They'd both vowed to communicate. And they'd learned how with the help of a counsellor right after they'd moved into Annabelle's home. At the end of the process, Max had promised to stick with her no matter what. As had she.

'Baba anakuja!' said Omar, and he gripped her hand even tighter.

Annabelle glanced up, her eyes watering to see that 'Papa' was indeed coming towards them. It was the first time one of the boys had referred to Max that way, and she envisioned many more years of it as they all grew to know one another even more.

He came and stood in front of her, his gaze searching her face. 'You're sure this is okay?'

'Do you even need to ask? Hope will be so

happy to finally meet them. So will the rest of the family.'

Glancing down at the two kids flanking her, he then leaned in and kissed her, his lips warm with promise. A small giggle burst from Ahmed at the PDA.

'It means we'll have even less privacy.' He tucked a strand of hair behind her ear, the gesture making her smile.

'No, it just means we'll have to be more inventive.'

'More? I don't see how that's possible.' Luckily the kids didn't have a strong grasp of English yet, but they would learn. Just as they would learn about their own heritage, possibly even returning to Africa one day to give back to their culture.

'You'll just have to wait and see. I have some ideas.'

Max leaned in and kissed her again. 'I think we'd better leave this topic of conversation for another time, or I'm going to be pretty uncomfortable on the trip home.'

Home.

Max had explained how seeing their wedding photo on her parents' wall had made something inside him shift, had made him realise he still loved her.

That picture now hung over their bed as a reminder of what they stood to lose. It was something that Annabelle kept in mind each and every day.

There were no more jokes about getting pregnant. She knew just how painful a subject it was, and she was more than willing to leave it behind. For Max's sake.

Besides, they were complete just as they were. Adding Omar and Ahmed to their household was just icing on an already beautiful cake.

And Nate… Her nephew's surgery had been a complete success, and there was no reason to think the brain tumour would ever return. Jessica was ecstatic, as was everyone else. It seemed they'd all got their happy endings.

It's enough.

Those two words were now the motto of her life. No matter what her problems or difficulties, she would weigh everything against that phrase. Because it was true. Life with Max, no matter what it brought, was enough.

She wanted to reach up and touch him, but the fingers squeezing hers prevented it. But there were other ways to touch. 'I love you.'

'I love you too, Anna.' He kissed her again before moving to the side and gripping Ahmed's hand, forming an unbreakable, unified line.

Then they walked towards the open door of the plane, knowing it would soon carry them to a brand-new phase of their lives.

Where they would wake up to face each and every day.

Together.

* * * * *